Western Fictioneers Presents:

𝕸olf 𝕮reek 10:
O DEADLY NIGHT

By Ford Fargo

Western Fictioneers

Beneath the mask, Ford Fargo is not one but a posse of America's leading western authors who have pooled their talents to create a series of rip-snortin', old fashioned sagebrush sagas. Saddle up. Read 'em Cowboy! These are the legends of Wolf Creek.

THE WRITERS OF WOLF CREEK, AND THEIR CHARACTERS

Bill Crider - Cora Sloane, schoolmarm

Phil Dunlap - Rattlesnake Jake, bounty hunter

Wayne D. Dundee – Seamus O'Connor, deputy marshal

James J. Griffin - Bill Torrance, owner of the livery stable

Jerry Guin - Deputy Marshal Quint Croy

Douglas Hirt - Marcus Sublette, schoolteacher and headmaster

Jackson Lowry - Wilson "Wil" Marsh, photographer

L. J. Martin - Angus "Spike" Sweeney, blacksmith

Matthew P. Mayo - Rupert "Rupe" Tingley, town drunk

Meg Mims – Phoebe Wright

Clay More - Logan Munro, town doctor

Kerry Newcomb - James Reginald de Courcey, artist with a secret

Cheryl Pierson - Derrick McCain, farmer

Matthew Pizzolato - Wesley Quaid, drifter

Robert J. Randisi - Dave Benteen, gunsmith

James Reasoner - G.W. Satterlee, county sheriff

Frank Roderus - John Hix, barber

Jacquie Rogers – Gib Norwood, dairy farmer; Abby Potter, madam

Jory Sherman – Roman Hatchett, trapper

Troy D. Smith - Charley Blackfeather, scout; Sam Gardner, town marshal

Charlie Steel –Kelly O'Brian, rancher

Chuck Tyrell - Billy Below, young cowboy; Sam Jones, gambler

L. J. Washburn - Ira Breedlove, owner of the Wolf's Den Saloon

Big Jim Williams – Hutch Higgins, farmer

THE WOLF CREEK SERIES:

Appearing as Ford Fargo in this episode:

"Sarah's Christmas Miracle"   Big Jim Williams
"Irish Christmas at Wolf Creek"   Charlie Steel
"A Home for Christmas"   Cheryl Pierson
"The Angel Tree"   Chuck Tyrell
"The Spirit of Hogmanay"   Clay More
"O Deadly Night"   Troy D. Smith

INTRODUCTION

In Wolf Creek, everyone has a secret.

That includes our author, Ford Fargo—but we have decided to make his identity an *open* secret. Ford Fargo is the "house name" of Western Fictioneers—the only professional writers' organization devoted exclusively to the traditional western, and which includes many of the top names working in the genre today.

Wolf Creek is our playground.

It is a fictional town in 1871 Kansas. Each WF member participating in our project has created his or her own "main character," and each chapter in every volume of our series will be primarily written by a different writer, with their own townsperson serving as the principal point-of-view character for that chapter (or two, sometimes.) It will be sort of like a television series with a large ensemble cast; it will be like one of those Massive Multi-player Role-playing Games you can immerse yourself in online. And it is like nothing that has ever been done in the western genre before.

This particular volume, and the previous one, are special: they are anthologies of stand-alone short stories rather than collaborative novels. We do that from time to time, to give our writers a chance to delve more deeply into their characters. When we sent out the call for Christmas stories, we got such a big response –including from many authors joining our Wolf Creek universe for the first time, with all-new characters –that we decided to release them as two normal-sized book rather than one giant one. So if you enjoy this volume, check out *Wolf Creek 9: A WOLF CREEK CHROSTMAS*, also on sale now.

You can explore our town and its citizens at our website if you wish:

http://wolfcreekkansas.yolasite.com/

Or you can simply turn this page, and step into the dusty streets of Wolf Creek.

Just be careful. It's a nice place to visit, but you wouldn't want to die there.

Troy D. Smith
President, Western Fictioneers
Wolf Creek series editor

SARAH'S CHRISTMAS MIRACLE

Big Jim Williams

"Hutch," cried Abigail, "Sarah's burning up. She may be dying...just like Robbie did."

"You sure?" asked her husband.

"Feel her head," pleaded a teary Abigail. "She can't die. It can't happen again...just can't."

Hutch placed a calloused hand on his daughter's forehead. "You're right. She is burning up."

Hutch and Abigail Higgins leaned over the bed of their five-year-old daughter in their small dugout home near Wolf Creek. Snow had been falling since noon and now at nightfall covered their farm with a thin layer of white, pushed by a churning wind.

"Snow on any other Christmas Eve would be welcome," said Hutch, "but not tonight."

"Maybe we should get her to Doc Munro?" asked Abigail.

"Honey, it's miles into town," worried Hutch. "Our old horse ain'tnothin' but skin and bones. Should of bought a couple of good ones after them damned Kiowas stole ours last week. Ain't sure this one'll make it to town. And I think a big storm's comin'."

"Can't we try?"

1

"Moving in cold like this might kill her."

"Sarah was so looking forward to decorating a Christmas tree and getting the pony we promised her," whispered Abigail. "Now..." She tried, but couldn't continue.

Hutch held his wife and kissed her on the cheek. "Maybe it can still happen. The livery stable's holding the pony I bought for her a couple of weeks ago."

"Oh, Hutch," cried Abigail.

"Let's give it a little more time," continued Hutch. "Try cool towels on her head. Maybe it'll bring down her fever."

"It didn't work with Robbie," choked Abigail. "Maybe if we'd taken him to Doc Munro when he got sick right after his second birthday he'd still be alive?"

Hutch didn't answer. Saying anything might provoke another argument, something he didn't need. He pulled on his hat, gloves, and old sheepskin coat. "I'll get some cold well water," he said. "Abby, let's try the wet towels...then we'll see."

***

An hour later, Sarah's head remained hot under the cold towels as she coughed and struggled to breathe.

"Hutch, she's worse," whimpered Abigail. "We can't lose Sarah, too. Just can't. She's still my baby."

"I'll get the horse and wagon," said Hutch. "It'll be rough goin'. Hope this snow don't get worse. You wrap her up good and tight in every blanket and quilt we've got."

Hutch grabbed his Henry repeating rifle and hurried toward the barn past their coop, which contained two wild turkeys. His eyes and heart looked toward a small mound and cross, silhouetted against the night and falling snow, on a slight rise beyond their barn.

"Can't let the same thing happen to Sarah," he said. "Can't." And if Sarah died, Hutch knew there would be two more crosses on the knoll, because Abigail wouldn't survive.

Inside their small dugout barn, Hutch lighted a candle lantern and quickly harnessed his old mare to the small wagon that had brought the newlyweds west after the War Between the States, to homestead in Kansas near Wolf Creek. He tied a horse blanket over the old mare, threw straw and old blankets onto the wagon bed, and created a half circle of grain sacks and empty boxes to protect Abigail and Sarah from the wind and cold.

Although decayed and torn, the wagon's canvas top would provide some protection. A wobbly rear wheel concerned Hutch. One spoke was missing and the rim was loose, but he couldn't worry about that now. He'd try to get Sarah to Doc Munro as fast as possible, although town was miles away.

After shoving his rifle under the wagon seat, Hutch moved to a barrel of grain, removed the top, and shoved his arm deep inside. He pulled out a leather sack. He cut the rawhide thong with his pocketknife and removed a cartridge-filled belt and two holsters with notched .44 Colt pistols, weapons with bloody histories best forgotten, but always remembered in the back of Hutch's mind.

"Wouldn't expect Kiowas out on a night like this," he said to himself, "but they might come back looking for food, warm blankets, scalps and killin'. Can't let that happen."

He reversed the holsters so the pistols were butt out—easier to grab while riding a wagon seat—and then buckled the stiff leather belt around his coat and waist. He checked to make sure the pistols were loaded.

Everyone who knew Hutch Higgins thought him a quiet, gentle dirt farmer. He was tall and lanky, in his mid-twenties, and unassuming—but Hutch, like so many in and around Wolf Creek, also had deadly secrets.

He bundled Sarah in layers of blankets and carefully placed her with Abigail in the cocoon of boxes and bags on the wagon bed.

The snowfall was a little heavier as Hutch urged his old horse slowly away from their soddy home onto the long, rutted, rocky path that led to the main road and help in town.

"This is a hell of a way to spend Christmas Eve," thought Hutch. "A hell of a way." He wished he'd bought the small Christmas tree in town and also brought back the pony he'd wanted to surprise Sarah with for Christmas.

He buttoned the top button on his turned-up coat collar, lighted his old corncob pipe, blew smoky warmth into his gloves before pulling them back over his cold hands, and settled onto the hard wagon seat.

"All right, girl, let's move, we got a long way to go and Sarah's mighty sick." Hutch slapped the old mare's haunches with his reins, but the stiff-legged animal didn't move. He slapped the reins harder, and the horse snorted and slowly moved forward.

Hutch's pistols revived bloody memories he preferred to forget. When he'd met Abigail months after the Civil War he'd answered her questions with, "No, I was too young to carry a gun for the Union. Stayed home in Ohio to help my Daddy run the farm after my three brothers marched off to war, and they weren't singing, 'Dixie.'"

Those were lies. No one knew Hutch's past, not even Abigail, and he wasn't about to tell her.

Hutch's parents had died from consumption on their dirt scrabble Ohio farm when Hutch was fourteen. Alone, and without any family or means of support, he wandered the land scrounging for work and food. Half starved and freezing during a cold winter, the shoeless Hutch threw his canteen and few belongings aboard a freight car stacked with sacks of grain. He didn't know where it was going, or care, as he burrowed among the sacks for warmth and munched on the cargo of oats and other grains. As the days passed, the weather became warmer as the train moved south. Hutch squinted through cracks in the freight car and began seeing rolling hills and forests, and then fields of cotton and tobacco tended by black men and women. Out of water and dying of thirst, he tore away a loose board on the side of the boxcar, waited for the train to slow, and jumped, landing in a tangle of briars and thick bushes. Within a mile he found a creek and drank until his stomach couldn't hold anymore. The warm sun felt good as he walked across the countryside, not knowing or really caring where he was. His pockets still contained some oats.

"I ain't starving," he said, "but I'm sure tired of eating oats."

He did find some wild blackberries, blueberries and plums that made life better. But watching out for cottonmouth snakes and sleeping with chiggers in the woods, wrapped in his mama's quilt, rapidly lost its appeal.

One morning, he was stopped by a group of armed riders. A red-faced man waved a coiled whip.

"Boy," he asked, "you seen any runaway slaves?"

"No, sir," shrugged Hutch. "Nothin' but snakes and chiggers."

"Chess Boy and his skinny no-account woman ran off sometime last night," said the man with the whip. "He's a big man,wearin' an iron collar. A ten-dollar reward if you see 'em. When I ketch that black bastard and his thievin' wench I'm gonna lash 'em good. Don't like slaves runnin' off, especially ones I been treatin' good."

The horsemen left a dusty trail as they galloped north.

Miles later, Hutch came across black men and women picking cotton under a hot sun.

He approached one of the stooped workers and asked, "Sir, do you know where a boy could get a job? I'm hungry and need work."

The slave looked up though startled eyes. "Who you callin' *sir*, massa? White boys don't go <u>sirrin'</u> peoples like me, not in a month of Sundays. You gotta be one of

6

those Yankees I keeps hearin' 'bout. But you doesn't look like a soldier."

"Ain't no soldier," smiled Hutch. "I'm from Ohio."

"You a runaway?" The man stood and rubbed his stiff back.

"Folks died. I'm on my own, but ain't had most nothin' to eat in days except some wild berries and plums and these oats." He showed some from his pocket. "Ain't crazy about eating horse food."

The slave chuckled and pointed down the road. "Them Fergusons might have somethin', but they's as poor as you looks."

It was the day the Ferguson family saved Hutch's life, and the day Hutch met Samuel "Champ" Ferguson, who changed his life in horrible ways Hutch couldn't forget.

***

Hutch turned on the wagon seat and said to Abigail in back, "How's Sarah?"

"She was coughing, but now she's sleeping," whispered Abigail from under layers of blankets with Sarah. "I think her temperature's down some, but she's still hot. How far have we come?"

"No more than a mile or two. A long way to go before hittin' the main road to Wolf Creek."

"Can't you go faster?" she pleaded.

"Not with this half-dead horse and a rear wheel about to collapse." Hutch felt and heard each turn of the wheel as it clunked against the washboard road. It was worse.

7

The plodding horse knew the road, but lacked the strength to move any faster. A thin layer of snow covered her blanketed back, Hutch, and the wagon's sagging canvas top.

Hutch sat hunkered over against the cutting wind. He stuffed his gloved hands in his coat pockets. The reins dangled at his feet. He wasn't worried about his horse moving too fast, he was worried the poor animal might drop dead any minute.

At one point the animal stopped to rest. Hutch patiently waited until it exhaled its frosty breath and decided to move. He knew he couldn't make the mare do more than she was capable of doing.

That's when he thought he saw three Indian riders in the distance. He couldn't imagine Kiowas out on a snowy Christmas Eve. They certainly weren't the Three Wise Men, but Hutch admitted he could use *their* help if indeed they were.

He nervously pulled the Colt cap-and-ball pistol from his left holster and confirmed it was still loaded. When he looked up again, the Indians, or whoever they were, were gone.

Tiny flakes of snow added another layer of white on the Kansas plains. On any other Christmas Eve Hutch would have enjoyed the quiet night, the crisp weather, and the growing blanket of white that stretched to the horizon.

The wagon slowly creaked forward; its old left rear wheel wobbled and sagged toward the ground as it continued to deteriorate.

When they finally reached the main road and turned right toward Wolf Creek, Hutch thought he saw the same three Indian riders in the distance moving parallel with his wagon. He rubbed his eyes, wondering if he might be seeing things through the increased snowfall.

He didn't mention his fear to Abigail.

The snow soon stopped and the moon broke through an opening in the clouds. The moonlight covered the land like a gigantic candle and turned the snow into an endless landscape of sparkling crystals and diamonds, a scene Hutch had never before seen.

"My God, that's beautiful," he softly muttered, not realizing Abigail was behind him. She wrapped her arms around Hutch and kissed him on his stubbled cheek.

"It is beautiful, isn't it," she agreed.

"How's Sarah?"

"Hutch, I'm scared. She's asleep, but needs Doc Munro, now. Her fever won't go down and she keeps coughing. And there's a rumbling in her chest. I think it may have turned into pneumonia."

Hutch patted her hand and chewed his lower lip.

Within a few hundred feet on the main road, as they crossed a small stream, the wagon's left rear wheel finally broke apart on the rocky creek bottom and the wheel-less corner hit the ground with a jolt. The wagon tilted and almost turned over. The old horse stopped in the shallow water and refused to move.

Hutch climbed down and checked the damage. "Dammit!" he said.

Abby peered from the back of the wagon. "Can you fix it?" she asked.

"Only with a jack and another wheel," sighed Hutch. "And we don't have either one."

"Can we still keep going?"

"I'll try, but I don't think our old horse can drag us and a three-wheel wagon out of here."

He coaxed, threatened and yelled, but the horse didn't move. He applied the whip, gentle at first, then harder. Final the old girl snorted, blew steam, and struggled out of the creek to the top of the rise. Then, on level ground, she gasped and collapsed in a tangle of harness. Hutch jumped down and knelt over the exhausted animal as it breathed its last breath.

He turned to Abby, now in the front of the wagon. "She's dead," he said, stroking the animal's neck. "She was old, but certainly gave all she had."

Abigail cried into her gloves. "Hutch, what are we going to do?"

"I gotta get to town and bring back Doc Munro. Can't wait here with Sarah so sick."

"You'd leave me?"

"There's no other way. We'd never make it carrying Sarah to town. It's miles. I can get there faster alone and bring help." He handed her one of his pistols and the rifle from under the seat. "You know how to use these. If any Indians should come, shoot 'em!"

She felt the notches on the pistol. "Where did you get this? I've never seen this pistol before."

"Not important," he said. "A long, long story."

10

She clung to Hutch and whimpered, "Don't go, please don't go."

"If I hear any shootin' I'll hurry back as fast as I can run. I gotta go, honey. You curl up with Sarah and stay warm. Be back as soon as possible."

He kissed his wife and daughter and hurried along the road to Wolf Creek.

***

It had also been cold that day in 1863 when Hutch helped Champ Ferguson and his Confederate raiders attack a small Tennessee border town. He had hung around the mountain community of Yankee sympathizers for a day before reporting back to Ferguson. Hutch easily moved through the divided pro-Union and Reb areas along the Kentucky-Tennessee border. Few paid attention to a kid whittling on a stick.

"Folks are both dead," replied Hutch, using a slight southern accent, if asked why he was on his own.

Hutch wanted to help the Confederate raiders since Champ Ferguson's family had saved him from starvation. At first he didn't understand what the Civil War was all about.

"The Fergusons are the only people, North or South, that ever gave a damn about me," Hutch would have said, if he were ever disposed to defend his actions. "Then after Champ's first border raid I found out all he wanted to do was kill anyone who supported President Lincoln or wanted to free the slaves."

Ferguson and his bushwhackers hit the Union border town in the late afternoon, shooting anyone who didn't get out of his way. He cut down people with his sword, men and women, old or young, it didn't matter to the Union-hater.

Whenever Champ used one of his two pistols to kill someone, he always notched a grip.

Champ enjoyed killing people, including captured Union soldiers, especially colored troops, something he did in a hospital until stopped by his own Confederate officers.

Hutch hid during the first attacks and then rode behind Ferguson when his cheering band fled back to their stronghold.

The raids continued, with Hutch scouting days ahead, before Champ Ferguson and his renegades struck for the Confederate cause.

"Why'd you have to kill that young unarmed man running across the street?" asked a teary Hutch after a raid.

"'Cause he's a damned Yankee!" spit Champ, cutting more notches in his pistols. "And Yankees breed more Yankees."

He hated anything Union, including a brother who was killed fighting for the North in the Kentucky cavalry.

Hutch thought Champ was worse than other Confederate guerrilla fighters like Bloody Bill Anderson or William Quantrill. The Fergusons had taken him in, but Hutch felt as if he had been *taken in*, not knowing of Champ's brutality.

Champ soon put Hutch on a horse, gave him a pistol and said, "I've helped you, boy. Now I'm gonna find out if'n you're gonna help me and the Southern cause.

You're ridin' on our next raid. And by God, either use that gun to kill Yankees or I'll be using mine...on you!"

Two days later, Ferguson attacked a small border settlement of pro-Union supporters. Hutch was there, his pistol drawn. He hesitated to fire until Champ placed the barrel of his pistol against the kid's sweaty head. "Hutch," he growled, "you either kill someone today or I'm leavin' you behind with a hole in your head. Do you understand?"

Hutched nodded.

Champ rode beside Hutch as they attacked the town. The raiders gave Rebel yells and killed anyone they saw on the street. They destroyed stores, wagons, and shot anything that moved.

Champ whirled his horse and grabbed Hutch's arm. "See that man yonder by that store," he asked, "that coward hidin' behind that barrel? You ride over there and shoot him...or I'll shoot you!"

Hutch hesitated until Champ cocked his pistol.

"Do it!" yelled the Rebel.

Hutch reluctantly nudged his horse across the street and stopped in front of the cowering man. He pointed his pistol, but hesitated, eyes filled with tears, until he looked back: Champ's big pistol was pointed at Hutch's head, and he never missed.

Hutch closed his eyes and fired at the shaking man. When he opened his eyes the man was face down in a growing pool of blood. Hutch felt sick. He looked toward Champ. Champ smiled and galloped down the street firing his pistol.

13

Hutch couldn't take it anymore. Within a week, he sneaked off late one night with Champ's two pistols, both notched with a record of Champ's brutality. He rode hard on back roads on one of Ferguson's best horses.

Hutch wasn't sad when the war ended in 1865 and Champ Ferguson was hanged for war crimes, tried for 53 murders. Newspapers reported Champ had "enjoyed" killing over a hundred people, something Hutch knew was true. Hutch read that the only other Confederate executed for war crimes was Captain Henry Wirz, who commanded Georgia's infamous Andersonville Prison where many captured Union soldiers starved to death or were shot if they crossed the prison's infamous *deadline*.

Hutch's time with Champ Ferguson was something he never planned to tell anyone about, especially Abigail. Some memories were better left buried.

***

Hutch's running to Wolf Creek soon slowed to a steady walk under light snow. Running made him sweat and sapped his energy. He'd forgotten to bring a canteen. He scraped snow off his hat brim and fingered it into his mouth. It helped, but hot coffee would have been better. It was a long way into Wolf Creek and he'd never get there if he collapsed in the road. He hoped he might meet a freight wagon or late night reveler, but didn't.

He was also concerned about what he thought were Kiowas. He kept scanning the bleak horizon as far as he could see in the dark, but no one was there.

He kept walking. Moving kept him warmer than standing still.

It was long after midnight when he spotted something in the middle of the road. Maybe a Kiowa trick? He drew his pistol, cocked it, and cautiously moved closer. Whatever it was didn't move. When he got closer he saw a saddled horse standing nearby in a gulley, its tail to the cold wind. There was no one else about.

Hutch crept forward. Whoever it was, was flat on his back, face coated with snow, jacket open, shirt and vest also covered in white.

"If he's dead," thought Hutch, "I'm riding his horse into Wolf Creek."

He nudged the body with the toe of his boot.

The body didn't move.

Hutch toed him again.

Then the man suddenly grunted. Startled, Hutch jumped back.

I think he's alive.

Hutch saw an empty bottle in the man's right hand and smelled the strong odor of whiskey. Then he noticed the man's left arm below the elbow was missing.

Hutched leaned over and, with a few waves of his hat, brushed off the man's snow-covered face.

"Well, I'll be damned!" gasped Hutch. "What in the hell is RupeTingley doing way out here?"

Rupe, Wolf Creek's most notorious drunk, spent more time sleeping off drunken binges in the jail than working as a swamper in the Lucky Break and other saloons in town. He reeked of alcohol.

Hutch shook him several times before Rupe snorted and opened one red eye. "Am...Am I...dead?" he asked.

"Dead drunk," replied Hutch.

"Well," muttered Rupe, "dead drunk's better...than being dead."

Hutched knelt and helped Rupe into a sitting position and asked, "What are you doing out here?"

Rupe opened his other eye, tried to drink from the empty whiskey bottle and then threw it away. "I need a drink."

Rupe's eyes slowly focused on his rescuer. "Hutch? That you?" he asked with a burp. "What in the hell...are *you* doing...out here?"

"That's the question I'm askin' you," replied Hutch, helping Rupe to his feet.

"Got in a fight with someone who pulled a knife...don't remember who...and rode out of Wolf Creek."

"That your horse?"

"Was under me when I left town...but I don't know how it got there...or who owns it. I must of fallen off. Damn! My good arm hurts."

Hutch hurriedly explained his desperate situation. "Rupe," he said, "I need to get back to my family, but if you're sober enough to ride back to town you can save my daughter's life. Get Doc Logan Munro to come as fast as possible and I'll buy you a case of whiskey! Tell Doc I think Sarah's got pneumonia, and to bring a fast

16

team of horses and covered rig so we can take her into town."

Although Rupe staggered, Hutch managed to get him back on his horse. "Can you do it, Rupe? I ain'tforgettin' if you do. If you can't, I'll take your horse and ride into town."

Rupe smiled: "For a case of whiskey...I'd ride this horse...to the moon."

"Take this bill of sale to the livery stable," ordered Hutch. "Tell Ben Tolliver to give you the pony I bought for Sarah. Then bring it back here. Her seeing it might do wonders. Now, git!"

Hutch slapped the horse's rump with his hat. "I'll buy you two cases if you hurry," he added with a shout.

"Yaaaahooo!" yelled Rupe, weaving in the saddle, kicking his horse into a gallop.

Hutch downed a big gulp of water from the canteen he'd taken off Rupe's horse, and trotted back toward his family. It was an hour later when he heard two gunshots that sounded like they came from the pistol he'd left with Abigail.

"Oh, my God!" he cried, using the last of his energy to race toward Abigail and Sarah.

The wind whipped the snow as an exhausted Hutch stumbled toward the wagon and saw, under the first rays of daylight, three Indian riders racing away from his wagon.

He fired twice, but missed.

He yelled Abby's name. There was no response. He climbed into the back of the wagon. Abigail and Sarah weren't there! All the blankets were gone.

Hutch panicked. "Those damned Kiowas! They've killed Abigail and Sarah. But Abigail would have fought them before letting them take Sarah. I heard two shots. Oh, God, this can't be happening."

The pistol he'd left with Abigail was gone, his Henry rifle still there. "Why didn't the Indians take the rifle?"

Frantically, he jumped out the back of the wagon. Abigail's footprints vanished along the side of the creek.

With more daylight he saw three different sets of moccasin footprints following Abigail's smaller ones. Then the larger prints turned and came back, the trail spotted with blood.

"Abigail! Abigail!" he shouted over and over as he ran along the rocky creek bed. A hundred yards away, he saw a brown mass against the side of the creek, his throat so dry and tight he could barely breathe. He moved toward the round pile. They were blankets. His blankets. Then the mound moved. Hutched yelled again:

"Abigail! Abigail! Abigail!"

The top of a blanket parted and there was Abigail's face, dotted with blood.

Hutch kneeled beside her and wrapped her in his arms. "The blood on your face? Are you and Sarah all right? What happened?"

"When I saw the Indians coming I grabbed Sarah and ran back here. I thought new snow would cover my tracks. When I realized it hadn't, I clawed my face, made it bleed, and dotted Sarah's face with blood.

18

When they came closer I fired my pistol twice. I wounded two of them, but they didn't stop coming. Then when they were only feet away I pointed to our bloody faces and yelled: 'Smallpox! Smallpox! Smallpox!' Those Indians turned and ran out of here like scalded dogs."

Tears cut through Abby's crimson face.

"Are you all right?" pleaded Hutch.

"I'm fine," she sobbed. "I prayed you'd come back."

"And Sarah?"

"I don't know." Abigail pulled back the edge of a blanket and revealed their daughter's blood-spotted face. She didn't move.

"Is she...?" choked Hutch.

"I don't know. She's been so quiet."

Hutch pressed his ear to Sarah's chest. "The rumbling's gone...and I hear a heartbeat." He ripped off his right glove and put his cold hand on her forehead. "Her temperature's down...feels almost normal. She seems better."

He told Abigail about meeting Rupe and sending him for Doc Munro.

"Rupert Tingley is the town drunk," she exclaimed. "How can you trust him to do anything right? He'll probably stop for a beer."

"I believe there's a good heart floating inside all that booze," said Hutch. "He'll bring Doc back if anyone can."

Then Abigail chuckled.

"What's so funny?"

"I'm remembering how those Indians looked when I yelled, 'Smallpox! Smallpox! Smallpox!' It was funny watching them race back down the creek and ride off.

"You can have your pistol back now," she added with a worried look. "Where did you get it? I'd never seen it before. Why so many notches? Hutch, did you kill people with this?"

"Only one, and it's not something I'm proud of."

"Then why all the notches?"

"I didn't put them there. An evil man did. Promise you'll never ask me about them again."

"But..."

"Promise!" he demanded.

"All right," she reluctantly said.

Hutch cleaned her face with snow and then kissed her.

The sun was up and bits of blue sky shown through the thick clouds when they were back inside the wagon. Shafts of bright light hit the wide expanse of snow-covered Kansas plain as wind suddenly caught some icy tumbleweeds and sent them spinning and dancing.

Sarah whimpered and opened her eyes. She looked up and said, "Mommy...is it Christmas morning yet?"

Abigail kissed and hugged her daughter. "Oh, yes, my darling, it is. A beautiful Christmas day with snow on the ground like you always wanted for Christmas. Lots of beautiful snow."

Tears streaked Abigail's smiling face.

Sarah frowned. "Mommy, why are you crying?"

"Because I'm so happy, so very, very happy."

A teary Hutch kissed his daughter.

20

"Daddy, do we have a Christmas tree?"

"With your bein' sick," replied Hutch, "I couldn't go to Wolf Creek." Then he smiled, "But...I've got an idea." He jumped out of the wagon, his exhaustion forgotten. He broke a long thin piece of wood from the side of the wagon and hammered it into the frozen ground using the butt of his pistol.

"Hutch, what are you doing?" gasped Abigail.

"Sarah," he said, "do you still want a Christmas tree?"

"Oh, yes, Daddy. Oh, yes."

"Then watch." Hutch did a little dance as he laughed and began singing "The First Noel" as he chased rolling tumbleweeds.

"Mommy, what's wrong with Daddy?"

"I don't know. He's just happy."

Both laughed as Hutch tried to catch wind-blown tumbleweeds.

He soon returned with tumbleweeds in both arms. He shoved the largest one over the stick, added a slightly smaller one, and then placed the smallest one on top.

"Mommy, has Daddy gone crazy?" asked Sarah.

Hutch sprinkled snow over his new creation. "This," he said to Sarah, "is the world's first tumbleweed Christmas tree."

Sarah giggled and clapped her hands with joy.

"But," continued Hutch, "with just a little help, your Christmas tree can also grow..."

He got two sticks from the creek and stuck them on opposite sides of his creation.

"...arms..." he continued.

Then he added two small dark pieces of wood to the top tumbleweed.

"...eyes...!" he exclaimed.

He ripped a small piece of cloth from his red bandana and shoved it in below the eyes. "...and a nose," he gleefully said.

He added his corncob pipe where a mouth should be and placed his hat on top of his tall masterpiece.

"Now, Sarah," declared Hutch, "your Christmas tree has become a snowman! What do you think of that?"

"Oh, Daddy, I love it." Sarah again clapped her hands.

Another shaft of light broke through the clouds and struck the snowman. Its snow-covered body also sparkled like diamonds.

"Oh, Hutch, it's beautiful," laughed Abigail. "Just beautiful."

Hutch opened his arms toward his daughter. "Sarah," he said, "say hello to your combination tumbleweed Christmas tree and snowman, that arrived just in time for Christmas morning."

"Oh, Daddy," she gleefully repeated, "I love it."

A man was driving hard toward them in an enclosed wagon. A mile behind came a lone rider swaying in the saddle. He led a pinto pony.

"It's Doctor Logan Munro and Rupe!" shouted Hutch, waving his arms. He turned and grinned at Abigail. "I told you Rupe could do it."

Doc Munro stopped his team alongside Hutch's wagon and jumped down with his medical bag.

"Hutch," he said, "Rupe tells me you got a mighty sick daughter."

"We sure *did*," replied Hutch. "She was real sick. Burnin' up with fever and couldn't stop coughing."

After several minutes with Sarah, Doc Munro, stethoscope in hand, emerged from their wagon, shook his head and said to the worried parents, "I don't know what happened, but whatever sickness Sarah had...is gone."

"We thought it was pneumonia," said Abigail. "Like our son, Robbie, when he died last year."

"Well," continued the doctor, "her chest is clear and strong with two good lungs. If she was sick before, she's fine now."

"A Christmas miracle," said Abigail. "Just what I've been praying for."

Doc Munro smiled, "It has been known to happen," he said, patting Abigail's hand.

"It was Rupe's doin' bringin' you here," acknowledged Hutch.

Hutch had Rupe tie the pony out of sight behind Doc's wagon. Rupe slid off his horse but hung onto his saddle until his knees stopped wobbling.

"Why bring the pony?" asked Doc Munro.

"Shhhh," cautioned Hutch. "It's a Christmas present for Sarah, so I don't want her to see it now."

"Oh, I understand," said the doctor with a wink.

"Rupe," continued Hutch, "You ain't ridin' the same horse you left with. What happened?"

"No, sir," grinned the drunk. "Ben Tolliver at the livery thought it best I ride one of his, 'cause someone with a hangin' rope's been lookin' for the thief that stole the one I was ridin'.'"

"We can't thank you enough for bringin' Doc," added Hutch, shaking Rupe's cold hand. "My offer to buy you two cases of whiskey still stands."

"Hutch," exclaimed Rupe, "I ain't had a drink since you sent me for Doc Munro. I'm thinkin' I may stop drinkin' 'cause it's Christmas."

Doc Munro and Hutch laughed. "That'll be the day," the doctor said, "though I'd love to see it."

"So," added Hutch, "you don't want the whiskey?"

"Now, hold on, Hutch," replied Rupe. "You don't have to buy me two cases, but I can always use a bottle or two. Kansas has lots of rattlesnakes, and a man should always have whiskey handy in case of snakebite."

***

Under a gentle snowfall, the five went to Hutch and Abigail's home where Abigail cooked one of their wild turkeys for a big Christmas dinner. Hutch gave the blessing, thanked God for Sarah's recovery, Abigail for being a wonderful loving wife, Doctor Munro for coming, and RupeTingley for bringing help.

Hutch placed the tumbleweed snowman outside the window where Sarah could see it, his pipe still in its mouth.

After singing Christmas carols together, the adults enjoyed a glass of Hutch's prized bottle of hard cider, while Sarah opened her Christmas present: a large rag doll Abigail had made.

Then, as a big Christmas surprise, Hutch presented Sarah with the pinto pony. She squealed and hugged its neck, her sickness long forgotten.

That cold, snowy winter of 1871 was a time of good food, laughter, thanks, love, music, and a Christmas miracle five Wolf Creek friends would never forget, especially a five-year-old girl named Sarah.

THE END

IRISH CHRISTMAS AT WOLF CREEK

Charlie Steel

Kelly O'Brian almost missed the Wolf Creek sign. It was at the dirt crossroad, indicating thirty miles ahead, and it pointed west. The gleam of the railroad track was off in the distance, just like the track Kelly had helped lay with his fellow Irish workers. Laying track was backbreaking work and, since collecting his pay and quitting the job, a few years had passed—years learning to hunt buffalo, skin hides, and ride a horse. He now had enough money saved to invest in a small ranch. Finished for good with slaughtering buffs since leaving the prairie and selling his last load of smelly hides, he was headed for the town of Wolf Creek. It was a growing cow town he had heard much about, a location where he hoped to find good grassland and water sufficient to start his own cattle ranch.

Powww! Boom! Powww! The explosion of different kinds of rifles sounded in the distance. This was no hunter or hunting party. The shots were too close together. Another volley repeated itself, and continued firing. Combatants with several different rifles were shooting at each other. Having served in the Great Conflict, Kelly knew the familiar sounds. One was a heavy bore Springfield muzzle-loader. Another was a large caliber Spencer, and still several others were those Henry repeaters.

Standing still, reins holding back Sage, his light colored buckskin, Kelly hesitated. The big horse had its

26

ears pricked in the direction of the gunfire. It quivered and sidestepped nervously.

"Easy, Sage," said Kelly, and reached down and petted his horse's neck.

Both horse and man listened as the firing decreased, and then stopped.

"Now a smart feller would ride in another direction," stated Kelly out loud to his mount. "Guess I'm not so smart."

Kelly O'Brian kicked his horse into motion and the land that was so seemingly flat had a slight rise before him. Horse and man climbed the hill and looked down. They saw in the distance a single covered wagon, and surrounding it were several riders. Two bodies lay on the ground. A wounded horse was on its side kicking long legs and raising dust.

"Well Sage, me boy," said Kelly in a soft tight voice that reverted to Irish brogue. "What you think we should be doing?"

The mounted horsemen were pointing their rifles, and a family was getting down from the wagon. First came a man, followed by a stout woman in a long dress. She stepped on a wheel hub and the man helped her to the ground. Then another younger woman was helped down, and last came a small boy. Even from that distance the shouting of the men, and crying of women, could be heard.

Dismounting, Kelly tied his horse to brush and pulled his Henry from its scabbard.

"Wait here, boy," he said, patting the horse's neck.

Kelly ran, using the rise of the hill for cover. When he arrived at lower ground, he hid behind brush as he advanced closer to the group. When he came up on the wagon, he stepped out. Rifle cocked and ready to use, he opened his mouth to speak and...

A heavy blow struck Kelly on the back of his neck. From the war, he was familiar with the strike of a rifle butt. For a moment he lost consciousness and did not remember falling. But when he awoke, he was on the ground, and a bearded old man with a Spencer rifle was standing over him.

"I knew it!" cackled the old man. "I saw him skyline himself. A twig broke and there he was. One of them no good job-stealing Black Irish from across the sea! I knows it; I can smell it in him. Good thing I parked the jail wagon back yonder!"

"Tie him up, Lester," said the leader of the group.

"Right, Jacob, I'll tie him up tighter than a turkey going to slaughter."

There were five tough men in all, four on horseback and the old man.

"Lester," ordered the leader. "You get the wagon and lock this lot in it. Don't dally."

"Jacob, I may be gettin old, but ain't no slower. I'll be back in a jiffy."

Kelly lay on the ground. He saw blood in the dirt and could still feel the trickle of it run down his neck and back. His neck hurt like blazes now, and there was no position he could get comfort. The old man had tied feet and hands tight enough to slow circulation, and his limbs tingled. While on the ground, he studied the family standing before him. The older, heavier woman was no longer sobbing, but tears—which she wiped away with a white

28

handkerchief—were still trickling down her face. Her husband stood silent beside her, arm around her shoulder. The daughter, long hair hiding her features, was close to the boy. When she suddenly turned at the snorting of a horse, he saw her face for the first time. She appeared no older than eighteen. The outlaws saw her too, and one of them gasped.

"A purty thing," said one of the men. "Wait till we get you back to the mine, girly."

"Shut your mouth, Stan," said Jacob. "She's for workin', not molestin'."

"Aww, Jacob, I was only funnin'."

"Mind your business and do as I say, or so help me, I'll put you in chains myself."

"Sorry boss, I'll..."

"Jessie, get down and drive that greenhorn's wagon," ordered Jacob. "You lead us out of here. We need all the wagons and mules we can get."

Jessie, one of the four mounted riders, rode over to the settlers' wagon. He got down, tied his horse to the rear, and climbed up on the wagon seat. Taking up reins, the man undid the brake and started the mule team forward.

The grating of steel tires on gravel sounded loudly, and then another wagon appeared pulled by four mules. It was what the old man called it, a prison wagon, a cage with a cover and thick steel bars all around, and built into the rear was a barred iron door. The old man got down and, producing a key, opened a big lock and removed a large chain. He opened the door and then chuckled loudly.

"All right you slaves, git in. Welcome to Lester's transport, compliments of the Jacob Coal Mining Company. Haw, haw, haw!"

With the pointing of rifles of the three mounted men, Kelly watched the boy, the older woman, the daughter, and father climb aboard. From the floor of the wagon, Lester took up shackles and came to Kelly and bent down, irons in hand.

"Now, you big Black Irishman," said Lester. "Don't you give me no trouble or I'll thump you another good one. I'll put these on your ankles and then untie you. Then youse hop on that wagon all by your lonesome. By the look of you, I bet you're strong enough to do two men's work."

As the old man stated, he put on the leg irons and then cut the leather straps from ankle and hands. Feeling the blood rush back into his hands and feet, the first time Kelly tried to stand up, he fell. Lester laughed.

"Bet you feel them pins and needles. Good, now up with you!"

The old man tugged on one arm, and Kelly found his feet. He stumbled to the wagon, the short chain jerking his feet, and then climbed up and sat down. Lester slammed the cage door, circled the chain, and fastened the lock.

"Where we going?" asked Kelly.

"Like I told ya," replied Lester. "Youse are all coal miners now! Haw, haw!"

One of the three riders separated from the party and rode up the hill and disappeared. In a short time he returned, galloping toward them, holding the reins of the Irishman's mount. As the vehicle jerked to a start, the prisoners in the wagon saw a horse, and the two dead men lying on the ground where they had fallen. Already buzzards began circling high in the sky.

"You didn't even bury my brother or my husband!" screamed the younger woman. "You—you—bunch of killers."

The wagon jolted and the long haired young bride lost her footing and fell. Two of the riders on either side of the wagon laughed. Now the father, on bended knees, full of grief, shouted out.

"If I ever get a gun in my hand, I'll…"

"You'll do nothing," said the leader in a hard cold voice. "Talk like that again, and you'll pay for it. This ain'tno game. Do as you're told and you'll live longer. Fight against us, and you'll suffer just like the others who tried."

Kelly O'Brian attempted to lean against the bars, but the jolting of the wagon bruised skin and bone. Pulling back, he lay sideways trying to become as comfortable as possible. There were following no road, and it looked to be some journey of unknown length. The big, heavy, barred wagon bounced and swayed as it drove over the prairie. Slowly, the heavy large wheels turned as they followed the lead wagon.

So, thought Kelly. *The pretty girl was already married and a widow.*

As he rode, he studied the family.

Her parents, smart enough to keep their mouths shut, rode in silence. From time to time they exchanged meaningful glances. The boy, who the girl called Billy, no older than twelve, sat with worried expression and stared

31

out the back of the wagon. The young woman, however, glared from one side of the wagon to the other at the riders, and if looks could kill, they would already be dead.

***

"Get moving, Kelly!" shouted the jailer, and then he cracked a whip across the Irishman's back.

It stung like crazy, and his shirt, already in rags, showed a back scarred with lash marks. A crew of over twenty laborers—all weakened by hard work, exposure, and poor diet—wearily swung pick axes and loaded wagons with coal. Every one of the men were pitch black of face, arms, and hands, their torn clothing all smudged dark by coal dust. What precious water the prisoners saw was for drinking, not bathing.

The first night they arrived, Kelly and the family were split up and locked into different underground tunnels. Kelly was thrown in a coal mine shaft and given bread and water. Locked in with him were dozens of men in various stages of health. All were weakening under the working conditions and it didn't take but an instant to understand. Either he would have to escape soon, or it wouldn't be long and he would be so weakened escape would be impossible. That is, except for the ultimate escape, death.

That night he tried his best to cope with the foul air of floating coal dust, and the strong smell of unwashed bodies. Kelly O'Brian panicked with a bout of claustrophobia. He had always hated enclosed spaces. Lying down, he sweated away his fear and then his mind would not shut off.

Not again, Lord! Not again! It's a terrible lot to be born an Irishman. This be just like before when me and

32

brother Shane escaped from Ireland on the awful cargo ships, locked into holds with little food or water—so many of us. I still hear the wailin' as bodies be thrown overboard to be eaten by the sharks. But what I can't abide and will never forgive myself is the death of me brother. Da, with his last starving breath, told me take Shane away from the cruel English Penal Law that robbed us of food and a decent life, and cross the ocean to America. But, Lord, forgive me. It was I that talked Shane into the Union and to join the bloody conflict. If I had it to do over again, Lord, it should have been me that took the wounds that did him in. I killed my brother. Lord above, if you recognize my thoughts and prayers, look over that family that was took captive with me. Especially, Lord, the wee bit of a girl who's too fair for the likes of this place.

What work the mother, the young woman, and the boy were given, Kelly wondered about. But occasionally the father was seen working in the pit alongside him, and only a few soft words and names could be exchanged before the whip from the overseer started cracking. How anyone could escape the armed camp and the guards with rifles on high ground, Kelly had no idea.

The mining operation was a surprise to the Irishman. It took a while, but finally he got the scope of the place. There was the single wide open pit that, with constant digging, expanded wider and deeper every day. A winding road led into the pit where teams of mules pulled wagons down into it. These were loaded, and then formed into caravans, to travel to various towns for sale of coal. Three distinct mine shafts with coal cars were constantly being lowered, filled, and brought up to dump into wagons.

Coal sold for only $3.50 a ton, Kelly knew this. But it appeared this was a more clever operation. Contracts to towns and ranches were being filled, and direct sales meant $80.00 a year or more per customer. There was very little wood in Kansas, and the poor burned twisted grass or dung. But, for those who could afford coal burning stoves, this ore was king. Supplying dozens of small towns with coal, and innumerable ranches, the profit would be great indeed. Whoever was behind this operation must be paying off the law or politicians. Still, for so many people to disappear into slave labor, must create some kind of mystery.

Kelly wondered about it, until he heard guards talking.

"I hear the boss raided a wagon train," said one of the jailers.

"Yeah, expect a whole passel of workers soon. We sure need 'em. This lot is getting tired."

"Read in one of the town papers, they blamed the Indians."

"That Jacob is too smart for the law," exclaimed another guard. "Slick work, no one's gonna question a thing."

Every hour seemed like a day to Kelly, and every day like a week. Already he was weakening. The gruel they fed in the morning, the watered down bean soup and moldy bread for lunch and supper, were not enough to keep a grown man healthy—let alone for the hard labor of a twelve-hour day. He learned those in the mines worked two separate shifts, and there the conditions were worse. There were cave-ins and occasionally men were injured or killed. Those who were injured or became ill were kept in a makeshift tent and watched by an armed guard. The women cooked food for both the guards and prisoners, and they also did the jailers' laundry. Every prisoner worked, and no one was left to idleness except for the sick and injured. Those who recovered were sent right back to work, and those who died were hauled off in a wagon.

One day, the boy from the family Kelly was captured with began going round with a bucket, serving water to guards and prisoners alike. Kelly, when it became his turn, whispered a few words.

"We got to escape, Billy. Tell your family."

"In one of the tents," whispered the boy. "There's a man who says he's your brother."

Kelly O'Brian was shaken right down to the soles of his feet. Deliberately he bent down and put the ladle back in the bucket.

"What's his name?"

"He says his name is Shane O'Brian."

A whip cracked.

"Here now, boy!" shouted a guard. "No talking! Back to work with you!"

The whip cracked near enough to the big Irishman that he could feel the air move against his back. Immediately he took up his pick and began breaking coal with repeated heavy blows. The boy lifted his bucket and offered the jailer a drink. The armed guard shook his head and the youth moved on to the next prisoner.

Kelly worked hard at breaking coal—harder than any day he had been there. His mind was finally off the pain of capture and being a prisoner. Now he had something else to think about.

35

*Somehow my brother is alive?*he thought.*But how? I saw my brother fall. It was I that carried his blood-soaked body to the surgeon's tent. Later, they told me he died and was buried. What they told me was wrong?*

All day long Kelly worked, swinging the pickaxe with a vengeance, and the guards looked on with awe and not a little bit of fear. At the close of the day, when the bell rang for the end of the shift, Kelly O'Brian was drenched in sweat and walked back to the tunnel to be locked in, and nothing about the man looked tired or weary after the long day's labor.

The floor of the mine was hard, and there wasn't anything soft to lie on but the clothing Kelly wore. The air was hard to breathe and the highest spot in the tunnel was up near the door. The big Irishman rose and walked nearer to it and lay down once more. There was just a smidgen of fresh air coming in from a space at the bottom.He turned sideways trying to lie as comfortably as he could, and his mind never left the troublesome thoughts he carried inside himself.

***

Slowly, with the help of young Billy Barber, the water boy, and his father, Claude, they formed a plan. One cool day in December, a guard, off duty and drunk, mislaid his keys. They were to the three mine doors that locked all the prisoners inside. That night, Billy, who stayed with his mother, stood in line to be locked in. Shielded by her dress, he snuck off into the rocks. At two in the morning, the youth crept to the mine and, with a heavy iron bar, crushed in the head of a sleeping guard. Undoing the lock and chain of the outer barred metal door, Billy opened the inside wooden door. Kelly was there and waiting. The boy, now wearing the guard's coat and gun, led the big Irishman to the sick tent, and without hesitation, the former Union soldier put the dozing armed guard permanently to sleep. Stripping the dead man of belt with Navy Colt and knife sheath, the Irishman strapped it around his own waist and donned the guard's coat. The boy took up the guard's rifle and led Kelly to his brother. The Irishman lifted Shane O'Brian from his bed and, as years before, noted how little he weighed. Walking quickly, Kelly carried him far from camp.

"Is that you, Kelly?" murmured the sick man.

"It's me, Shane, me boy."

"I'm glad," said Shane.

"Me, too, brother."

"I'm afraid I'm awful sick," said Shane.

"That's all right. We'll get you better. You wait here while I get the others," he said, as he placed his brother gently on the ground.

Together, Billy and Kelly slipped back into camp. Another guard, sitting asleep by a different closed mine shaft, was swiftly dispatched by Kelly. Using one of the keys, Billy removed lock and chain and the heavy double doors were opened. Claude Barber stepped out and stripped the dead guard of coat and weapons. The tough older man followed them to where the women were kept, in another of the mine shafts. The process was repeated, and the third jailer was removed of his life and possessions, and Mrs. Helen Barber and daughter Elizabeth were freed.

Behind Elizabeth followed two black-haired women. Even in the dark they appeared to be Indians.

"Who are they?" asked Kelly in surprise.

"Friends of mine," replied Elizabeth. "Sawni and Little Spring—they helped mother and me. I'm not going without them."

"They could hold us up," said the Irishman.

"No, they'll help us. Little Spring is Cheyenne, and she wants to go back to her people. And Sawni is half-black/half-Seminole and she wants to go to Wolf Creek with us. I promised both of them that since they helped us, I would help them."

"All right," whispered Kelly. "But be quick about it."

As the four women followed the Irishman out of the shaft, Sawni and Little Spring began to gather blankets from the dead guards' possessions.

There was no guard for the horses. Kelly looked for his mount, but Sage was not in the corral and nowhere to be found. While the horses were being saddled, Kelly smothered his disappointment at not finding his favorite animal. Upset, he found his way back to the open mine shafts and woke several of the prisoners in each cavern. The doors still open, and with no discovery, he repeated the same message.

"What you do for your freedom is up to you, but be quiet about it," he said, then Kelly O'Brian hurried back to the corral.

Taking the reins of two saddled horses, Kelly cautioned the others to walk their steel-shod animals quietly from the camp. When they came to where Kelly had laid Shane, he picked his brother up and put him in the

38

saddle. Then he led the horses further from the mining camp. When he thought they had gone far enough, Kelly gave the signal and they mounted and rode away into the night, heading west.

When they had gone several miles they began to hear shooting. Having no idea of the outcome of the other captives' escape, they continued on through the night and into the next day. When night fell once more, they were more than thirty miles from the mine. They camped before a water hole and Kelly shot a deer. Within minutes the animal was cut up by the two Indian women, and the meat was collected in its hide. Snuggled in the guards' blankets, they sat around a small fire while the meat cooked on sticks. For the first time since capture, the former prisoners feasted until they could eat no more.

***

Shane O'Brian remained sick and could not be moved further.

"The rest of you travel on," said Kelly. "Don't let me hold you up. The other guards may come looking for us."

No one in camp would leave. Finding and making remedies, the two Indian women put it in Shane's water and he drank the bitter brew. Through a day and night the health of the young Irish immigrant lay in balance between life and death. His fever would increase and then lessen and every hour the two women tended to him. They kept him warm with extra blankets and coaxed him to drink fluids, some with the willow bark medicine they prepared for fever.

In the morning the fever broke and, for the first time, Shane ate some venison stew. Kelly killed another deer.

They cooked the meat, ate, and the Indian women wrapped the rest away for the future. Saddling and packing their few possessions, they again headed west.

"Shane," said Kelly, riding beside his brother. "I been meaning to ask you…"

"You want to know how I'm still alive after Bull Run," replied the brother in a raspy and weak voice.

Kelly rode closer and as the horses walked side by side, the big Irishman bent near to hear his brother's words.

"When I woke, I was out of me head, didn't know who I was for a long time. They took me to some house and slowly I recovered from my wounds. Still, my mind was foggy and the Union discharged me. One fellow I was with wanted to go west so I went with him. We got off the train and got work. When learning to ride I took a fall and then me memories came back, all of a sudden I knew my name. I'm sorry Kelly, but I didn't want to go back to the war, so I stayed where I was. After the conflict ended, and while I was headed back looking for you, I was captured by that bunch of slavers."

"It's all right Shane," replied Kelly. "I'm so bleeding glad to see you that no words can—you just stay warm and try to recover your health."

"I've been awful sick brother. The food and the work took me off my—"

"Don't you worry," said Kelly. "I've got a bit of money saved, and if you're in favor, we can be buying a little ranch to raise cattle."

Shane smiled broadly for the first time since Kelly had seen him.

"Brother," said Shane. "It was a cattle ranch I worked on and I was a right smart cowhand. If you be looking for a partner I—"

Kelly laughed, and thrust out a right hand. Shane took it and shook with what strength was left in him.

Kelly, not paying attention, led the group down a slope and then back up a rising hill. As if the ground itself produced them, a large bunch of painted Indian warriors instantly appeared all around. The leader rode a nearly white mustang and he was the only one not holding a weapon. Some thirty warriors pointed rifles at their group, and Kelly noted wide-bore .58 Percussion Springfields carried by half, and the remainder had Henrys. How these mounted warriors managed the ambush without firing a shot put the fear of God in the Irishman. To come so far and survive so much danger, to be so near their goal and to fail, galled Kelly to no end. For surely death was near, and from the looks of it, a slow and painful one.

Then Little Spring came from behind and started talking in a language none of them could understand. The leader of the group grunted, stepped his light horse closer and responded. The Indian chief spoke an order and rifles lowered.

"This is my father, Strong Horse," the Cheyenne woman declared.

The captives made a collective sigh. There was a long conversation between father and daughter in their own language. The Indian on the light horse began to speak in a loud firm voice. Little Spring translated.

"Father says you have strong medicine to come from far across the great waters to find and save his daughter.

41

He says you have even stronger medicine to overcome his vow to kill all whites. Move close and he will give you a token, so that all will know you are spared by the People."

Kelly rode his horse near to the Cheyenne chief, and with a quick movement the older Indian took up an amulet from around his neck and quickly placed it over the white man's head. The chief spoke again.

"This will give you safe passage," translated the girl. "The whites steal the People's land. Before they take all that is ours, we fight back. Now go! "

Without hesitation, Kelly started his horse and hoped that those behind him would follow. From the corner of his eye he saw Little Spring raise her right hand high, palm open. When they had traveled a safe distance, Kelly stopped and the Barber family and the other Indian woman, Sawni, circled round.

"Whew! Good thing we had her along," said Kelly.

"I told you Little Spring would bring us luck," said Elizabeth.

"Was that her name?" asked Claude.

"She told me that is what her name meant."

"I say it fits," said Shane.

Not stopping to rest at noon, the party rode on.

"Wolf Creek should not be far from here," Kelly informed them.

It was getting colder; clouds were gathering and darkening before them. The wind increased and blew hard from the north, and then snow began to fall. Riding beside his brother, Kelly could see Shane's face was flushed with fever and he was beginning to cough. Shane was still weak from his ordeal and this cold wasn't helping.

From a side trail, through increasing snowflakes and blowing wind, appeared another rider. It was a cowboy.Around his head, holding down his hat, was tied a scarf.

"Howdy," said the cowhand. "My name's Jimmy Spotted Owl and I'm headed for town! You folks look mighty chilled!"

Kelly stopped his horse and in a few words he told the cowhand his name and explained their ordeal.

"Follow me, folks," called Jimmy. "I'll get you to Wolf Creek and find you a warm spot and some vittles. You all know what day this is?"

The group shook their heads.

"Well, glory be!" shouted Jimmy through the wind and blowing snow. "It's Christmas day!"

Jimmy took the lead and hurried his mount up the now-hidden road. If anything, the wind blew stronger and colder, and Kelly, taking a blanket, tried to wrap it round his brother. Shane's face was now beet red, and he was coughing non-stop. Through growing drifts, the cowhand led them into town. The wind was now blocked by buildings and it was easier going. Understanding that one man was badly ill, Jimmy led them past mercantiles and a saloon, to a doctor's office. There was a little sign on the glass door that said *Logan Munro, M.D.*

Jimmy dismounted and through the blowing wind shouted out.

"You just get down and pound on that door. The Doc can be temperamental but don't take no for an answer. Mister Kelly, you just tell him your story and I bet my life he'll help. I'll take your hosses and stable them and then look for Sheriff Satterlee, so you can tell him about that coal camp. Being the day it is, it might be hard to find him. Give me a little time, but I guarantee to fetch back some Christmas spirit."

Kelly nodded his head in reply.

"Me," said the Indian girl. "I go with you. I look for Charlie Blackfeather, he is kin of mine. You know him?"

"I sure do, but I haven't seen him around, ma'am."

"No *ma'am*, my name's Sawni, it means echo."

"Well, Sawni, let's take these hosses, before we freeze to death."

Dismounted, Kelly reached up and took his frail brother bodily from his horse. Then he led the Barber family up the steps to the doctor's door. Kelly, his brother still in his arms, tried the door handle. It was locked. Pounding loudly and without stopping, each time with more force, the frozen door began to rattle and snow fell from its window panes. Finally, the door opened.

"What's all the pounding about?" complained Dr. Munro. "Do you know what day it is?" The doctor looked tired.

Forcefully, Kelly, still holding his brother, pushed his way into the warm room. From behind, the Barbers, equally chilled, also pushed their way in and the doctor had to back across his office.

"What the…" began the Doc, but he had no opportunity to finish.

Kelly, carrying his brother, shoved the doc into the next room. Finding a cot, he laid Shane upon it, all the time explaining their long ordeal and the reason for his brother's ailment. The Doc took a deep breath, absorbed

44

the details of the message, and—dropping his bluster—asked a question.

"Ma'am," Dr. Munro said to Helen Barber. "I'd like a little help, are you up to assisting me?"

"Doctor, my name's Helen, and as soon as I'm warm and wash my hands, I would be glad to help."

"Then good," said the Doc. "The rest of you clear out of here and into the next room."

Claude, Elizabeth, and Billy Barber did as they were told. Kelly hesitated and the doctor looked up at the tall Irishman.

"Well, go on," said the Doc. "You did your part, now it's my turn."

Time passed, and the front office was warm as toast. The Barber family and Kelly removed their outer clothing to reveal the rags they were still dressed in. Kelly hadn't noticed before, but Claude Barber had what looked like a heavy cloth bag that he was nervously clutching. Kelly wanted to ask, but the condition of his brother weighed hard upon him. Elizabeth came over and sat by Kelly and she touched his hand and began to speak.

"I haven't had a chance to thank you for all that—"

Then the front office door opened and through it burst Jimmy the cowboy, all smiles and his arms full. Behind him came the Indian girl carrying a number of tied packages. The smell of warm cooked food immediately permeated the small room.

"Merry Christmas!" shouted Jimmy. "Sawni and me took care of the mounts and then we had a dickens of a time finding Christmas dinner. Everybody's celebrating and shops are closed and—"

"Jimmy is a funny man," exclaimed Sawni. "He go to Li Wong's Chinese Laundry. He talk, talk, talk. Finally he get roasted duck, soup, beans, pie, all for us."

"I told them your story," explained the grinning Jimmy. "And when I did that, they gave us their cooked dinner. 'Course, a gold coin or two helped."

"I'll pay you back," said Claude Barber.

"No need," replied Jimmy. "It's Christmas, and I would have blown it anyway. Besides, if you folks don't mind, I can enjoy the day with you and the lovely Sawni. It beats getting drunk in a saloon."

The young Indian woman smiled, snow white teeth flashing in contrast to her dark hair and honey-colored skin. Then she dropped her head and quickly raised it again, the gleam of affection in her eyes.

"Told you!" she said. "Jimmy Spotted Owl, real funny man. Like many Cherokee men."

"A real hard-working Cherokee cowboy is what I am, and proud of it, too! Say! What Christmas would be complete without a little libation? I went to the saloon, and it took some doing, but I brought back a bottle of whiskey. Not the cheap rotgut, mind you, but an honest-to-goodness real bottle of whiskey!"

The inner office door opened and Dr. Munro came out, followed by Mrs. Barber.

"Your brother's got some congestion, but my professional opinion is he'll make it," said the Doc. "Providing he stays here, keeps warm, and rests for a few days. He needs food and care. It took him a long time to get this run down, and it will take some time to recover."

"Anything I can do, Doc?" asked Kelly. "I can pay—"

"We'll discuss that later," replied Dr. Munro. "Right now, I'm late for a date and Christmas party. Being what day it is and the cold outside, I recommend all of you stay here. Enjoy the dinner Jimmy brought you, and camp out on the floor. Judging from your appearance, I imagine this will be a luxury for you. Jimmy, I trust you to watch the place for me."

The Doc disappeared. Pulling a small table to the middle of the room, Elizabeth and Sawni began unwrapping food. In a short while all of them were filling their bellies. Kelly went into the inner office and gave Shane a bowl of soup.

"Say, brother," said Shane. "The Doc gave me this paper to read. Look, there's a ranch for sale. Five thousand acres, buildings, springs, a little lake, plenty of grass—"

"How much?" asked Kelly.

"It says here, five thousand."

Kelly hung his head.

"Sounds perfect, but I don't have that much."

The group from the outer office crowded in around Kelly and Shane.

"I heard that," said Claude Barber. "You may not have it, but I do!"

"But how?" asked Kelly.

"When you went back to free the other prisoners, I searched and found my wagon," replied Claude. "I had this hidden away."

Claude Barber held up his heavy bag of coins.

"I have some money hidden in the lining of my belt and the rest back in a bank in St. Louis," said Kelly. "If you're interested in a partner, I could go half."

"It would be my pleasure," replied Claude, holding out his hand.

Kelly took it and shook hard.

"You fellas better make the deal quick," Jimmy Spotted Owl said. "Andrew Rogers has been buying up every lot that comes open. And I'd lots rather see you get it than him, the snake."

"Looks like we'll do so," Kelly said.

"Time to celebrate!" said Jimmy, handing Shane a glass with amber liquid. "Take some good medicine."

With the help of Sawni, more glasses and cups were handed all around. Then Jimmy poured whiskey for each of the group.

"I don't think the Doc will mind," declared Jimmy. "I suppose a little snort wouldn't hurt your brother. It might even help."

Solemnly, Claude Barber raised his drink and everyone followed his example.

"Here's to new friends and a Merry Christmas!"

"And a Happy New Year!" declared Elizabeth.

The patient held the drink, and then upended it. Claude, Helen, Elizabeth, Sawni, Jimmy, Kelly, and even Billy, joined him.

"Now folks," said Shane, between a cough and a smile, "This is what I call a grand Irish Christmas."

THE END

A HOME FOR CHRISTMAS

Cheryl Pierson

The Reverend Dill Hyder was never pleasant to be around, and this holiday season seemed to have brought out the worst in him.

The Methodist parsonage had become so fraught with tension that Kathleen had just had to escape. *Especially after what she'd done.* Their little dwelling was small, even on Dill's "good" days; on days like today, the walls seemed to close in so tightly they sucked the life out of the tiny abode.

The snowfall had stopped yesterday afternoon, but more was on the way by the feel of the air—the blessed outside air that cleared Kathleen's mind and allowed her some sanity once more.

When she'd broken the news to her husband that she would be visiting her dearest friend, Elizabeth Jenkins, for Christmas rather than spending it with him, he had turned red with fury.

"A husband and wife should not be separated during these holy days of Christmastide, Kathleen," he'd stated with a self-righteous sniff. "I forbid it."

"Nevertheless, I am going," Kathleen replied, meeting his cold, fish-eyed stare.

"A wife's duty is to be obedient." Anger lit his eyes, though he tried to mask it. He glanced down when Kathleen didn't look away.

"Not my strong suit, husband," Kathleen replied succinctly.

His head snapped up, face mottled. "You're lucky I took you back after you were kidnapped! What I've been through—for your sake—and yet you are wholly ungrateful. Five years of marriage I've given you, hoping and praying to our merciful Father that you would repent of your headstrong, defiant ways and become a dutiful wife as God commands! You've brought me nothing but shame—from not being able to conceive a child to being used by those renegades who took you—"

Something had broken and twisted inside Kathleen's soul at that moment. The high-handedness of his expression and the venom of his words had shattered her heart, but not her spirit, and not her backbone.

She'd done something then that had sealed her fate, but she could never ever regret it. She'd drawn back her fist and delivered a right cross that any of her brothers would have been proud of. No dainty slap for her. The blow she'd given the pastor had knocked him 'asshole over teakettle', as her father would have said—and given him a black eye he'd still be trying to explain. But it was the culmination of years of frustration, of belittlement, and starvation of her soul at Dill Hyder's hands.

They'd not spoken a word the next day, nor the day after. Now, here she was on her way to visit Elizabeth who lived in Maryville, the nearest town to Wolf Creek...and Elizabeth had no idea she was coming.

Kathleen pressed her lips together, holding the reins tightly as the buggy moved along at a good speed for the road conditions.

She wasn't worried, she told herself, casting another quick glance skyward.

If the weather would only hold until she reached Elizabeth's home, she would not care how deep the snow fell afterward.

Her eyes stung at the thought of her predicament. *What would she tell Elizabeth and her family? That she and Dill were at odds?* At odds. Much more than that. Her marriage was over, and now she wondered why it had taken her this long to realize it.

From the corner of her eye, she caught a glimpse of movement to her right. A noise came to her, faintly, and had conditions been otherwise, she might not have heard it at all. She pulled back on the reins, bringing the small conveyance to a stop.

She looked back toward where she'd seen the movement. Under the barren branches of the winter woods, the figure of a man lay half-buried in snow.

She hesitated but a moment before climbing down from the buggy. She reached for her muff that served a dual purpose on this miserably cold day—keeping hands warm, as well as concealing a small pepperbox derringer. After being kidnapped and held hostage only a few weeks earlier, she had vowed to be prepared for anything once her brother Derrick had come to her rescue.

But Derrick had no idea she was heading for Elizabeth's home.

She started forward, worried that the man may have already succumbed to the elements, apprehensive that he had not.

As she drew closer, she could see the smear of deep red close to his left foot.

He lifted his head, anguish written across his dark features.

Kathleen stepped closer, relief flooding her as she recognized him. "Carson? Carson Ridge?"

He gave her a half-smile, and the worry dissipated— but not the pain. "Kathleen!" He tried to sit up, but gasped and bit back a curse.

"What are you doing here? What happened?" She hurried forward to stand close beside him.

"Trap," he said shortly. "My dog—got caught. I got him out, but there was another nearby, under the snow. I was on my way to Derrick's—Christmas, you know—" He broke off in a grimace as he leaned forward to try to see the damage the trap had caused.

Kathleen had already bent to look. The steel jaws of the trap had been forced apart partially. Blood froze on the sharp teeth. *Carson's blood.* She shuddered.

"You're almost free of it. Let me help—"

"Be careful," he panted. "I don't want you getting hurt."

Kathleen's eyes stung suddenly at Carson's words. So different, he was, from Dill—the man she'd sworn to love, even though he'd never said anything half so kind to her in their five years of marriage.

She nodded, turning away to hide her emotions. "I will be careful," she said, regaining her composure.

"If you can manage to pull up on the top part, I'll pull down and get my foot out. Just—just be sure to let go quick."

"Once you get your foot out—" she clarified unnecessarily.

That brought a pained chuckle from him. "Not one second sooner."

She blushed, realizing how silly she'd sounded. "Ready?" she asked, wrapping her fingers around the gnarled metal.

"*Past* ready," he muttered, trying to grip the bottom half of the trap.

"Let me," Kathleen said gently. "I can pull it apart. You've broken the spring." She placed both hands on the trap.

He nodded, because he had no choice. But the worry in his dark eyes touched her.

"Kathleen—"

"It'll be fine. We'll have done with this and get you someplace warm."

True to her word, she pulled the trap open, allowing Carson to get free of it. Releasing it, the trap closed, but not with the speed and danger it had once held.

Carson rolled over in the snow and lay still. His breathing was shallow and ragged.

"Carson?" Kathleen's voice was a hoarse whisper.

"I'm okay," he answered. "Just had to get my breath."

Kathleen nodded, though he couldn't see her. "Your dog—"

"Oscar. He's here." He turned to face her, and sat up with a grimace. "His foot's hurt, but I think it will mend." There was uncertainty in his voice. "He's been trying to circle me and protect me, but he wouldn't be able to help much."

"I'll get the buggy down here closer so you don't have to walk so far on your foot."

Carson eyed the distance to the buggy, then gave her a regretful look. "You won't be able to pull it off down here. You'd never get it back up the hill in this snow."

"Can you even put weight on your leg?" She didn't want to say any more. She'd known Carson since childhood. He and her half-brother, Derrick, had been inseparable, until the McCain family had pulled up stakes and moved north, to Kansas. She knew just how stubborn Carson could be—he was the only person she knew who could stand equally with her brother when it came to determination.

"We're going to find out…" His voice trailed away as he shifted to try to stand.

Kathleen hurried to his side and he looped an arm around her shoulder. She floundered for an instant, slipping in the snow before she was able to dig in her heels and hold both of them upright.

But, somehow, after the first few halting steps, she knew she'd been right about his grit; if anything, it had only gotten stronger over the years.

They made it to the buggy after an interminably slow climb up the gently-sloping embankment.

Carson leaned against the conveyance, taking his weight off Kathleen's shoulders, smiling as she drew in a deep breath. His coal-dark eyes lingered on her for an instant and the silence became awkward.

"What are you thinking, Carson Ridge? Might as well spit it out—you deviled me enough as a child—have you forgotten how?"

He shook his head and started to climb into the buggy awkwardly, favoring his injury. "I was thinking about the time you were chasing Derrick and me, and you ran through the patch of sand burrs."

Kathleen put a hand out to help, but didn't touch him. He was managing—and he might resent it.

"I remember," she said quietly. "You came back for me. Carried me out of the field." She could still feel the way his hands had grasped her, how he'd slung her around to his back gruffly, as if he hadn't wanted to be bothered. But he *had* come back for her, when her own brother hadn't. And though he'd chided her as a much older ten-year-old, her childish eyes had idolized him from that moment on.

He gave a long whistle, his eyes scanning the woods nearby for the injured dog. "Well, *somebody* had to do it." He flashed her a grin. "You might still be out there in the sticker patch if I hadn't come to your rescue."

A faint bark came from the dark woods, and Carson relaxed against the leather seat. "Or, worse yet, someone else might have saved you."

Kathleen gave a short laugh. "Not much chance of *that* happening. Even my own brother ran off and left me."

"But he came for you when it counted, Kathleen. At Demon's Drop. He was ready to give up his life to save yours."

She nodded, looking toward the woods, thinking of how Dill had thrown up her kidnapping to her time and again. Yes, Derrick had come for her when it was most important—when she never dreamed he would. When her own husband as much as said it would have been better had she died at the hands of the outlaw gang. She and Derrick had never been extremely close. Though she'd hoped he would track her kidnappers and rescue her, she hadn't held out much hope that it would happen. But it had.

"I trust things are better between you two now? Derrick's always been a stubborn one."

Kathleen met his eyes. "Yes. He and I have—sorted things out. I wish we'd been able to talk about it all sooner; that it hadn't taken a kidnapping to bring us close again."

"Oscar!" Carson called. The dog came as quickly as he could, one of his back paws trailing spots of blood in the whiteness. He pulled it up and ran on three legs.

Carson leaned down to boost him up into the floor of the buggy.

"Your horse—where is he?" Kathleen lifted her snow-caked skirt to climb into the seat next to Carson.

"He took off. I just got him last week so…he doesn't know me that well yet to care if we ride together or not."

Kathleen took up the reins. "We can't just leave him out here. We'll be getting more snow soon." She reached into the compartment behind them and brought out a soft, warm blanket. "Here, let's put this around you—"

"I'm too bloody. It'll ruin this—"

She shook her head. "*You're* more important to me than a *blanket*, Carson."

A smile tugged at his lips, despite the tightness in his expression. "I don't believe anyone's ever told me that before," he teased. "Sounds kind of romantic."

Kathleen rolled her eyes. "There's a first time for everything, they say. And I'm not sure I would even remember how to say anything romantic to anyone at this point…even if I weren't a *married lady*, Mr. Ridge." She tucked the blanket in around him, but he spread it cross her lap, too.

"Don't worry about that horse," he said when she gave him a quick look. "He's smart. He'll find the nearest place that smells like food."

***

Kathleen drove in silence, trying to think of what to do. Take him back home with her? A wry smile touched her lips. *How the Reverend Hyder would hate that*. Barely able to stomach anyone of color, he'd as leave sleep in the barn than offer a Cherokee Lighthorse officer a bed under the same roof.

They could press on to Elizabeth's…but Kathleen was unsure as to how her friend's family might react to Carson. Kathleen had never known nor understood such prejudices, having spent her childhood in the Cherokee community of Briartown, her father the Cherokee school's white headmaster.

The snow had begun to fall, as she'd known it would. Carson had long since passed out—a testament to the pain he'd hidden so well in the beginning. The wolf-dog lay beside him under the blanket.

They would not make it to Elizabeth's, and there was no turning back. Of the few small homesteads dotting this section of the road, the nearest was Josiah Maxwell's place. An inhospitable, dour older man, Kathleen wondered if he would let them in the door.

The snowfall was increasing. She had to do something. She peered through the gray afternoon, seeking the fence posts that marked Maxwell's property.

Finally, she was able to make out the first one, and her heart raced. A few moments later, she was turning off the main road toward the small cabin, relief thrumming in her veins. *How could he turn them away? Surely, he wouldn't.*

As she approached the front porch, she saw a sleek paint standing beside the cabin, its saddle and gear intact. It had to be Carson's.

She pulled up to the front steps and put the brake on the buggy. Pushing the blanket off of her lap, she climbed down and called out. "Hello? Mr. Maxwell?"

She carefully started up the ice- and snow-covered steps, knocking on the door. The cabin looked deserted. Surely, if he'd been here on this dreary day, he'd have a fire going. But there was no smoke billowing from the chimney, no light from inside spilling through the windows.

She pounded on the door again. "Mr. Maxwell? It's Kathleen Hyder. Would you please open the door?"

After a moment, she tried the handle and the door swung open with a creak.

It was plain to see that Josiah Maxwell had gone…and not just for a short trip. Everything about the small homestead spoke of a permanent leaving. As Kathleen walked into the front room, a note on the dining table nearby gave the proof.

I have gone to Texas and will not return.
I bid you farewell.
> *December 20—1871*

Two days ago.

Kathleen dropped the note back onto the wooden surface and hurried back outside. They were here, she and

Carson. There was shelter for them, and for the animals. They were safe.

Now, if she could only get Carson inside…If she could get him to the bed…If she could get a fire started…get the animals safe in the barn…see to Carson's injury—and Oscar's too—she would not let the poor animal be in pain.

So much to do, but the hardest part was over. There was safety here, and that was the main thing. They were going to make it.

***

Carson came to with a shout that shook the walls of the small bedchamber. The pain jarred him from peaceful unconsciousness to painful present—an unfamiliar place, with the Angel of Fire standing over his injured foot, holding an open bottle of whiskey.

Bleary-eyed, it took him a moment to realize that the blonde woman at the foot of the bed was certainly no angel—not with that bottle of fire water she was pouring over his mangled foot.

"Dammit!" he roared.

She stepped back, not in fear, but as if she wasn't certain if he was fully awake, cognizant or his actions.

"Oh…I'd hoped you'd still sleep through that," she said.

"Not likely!" He tried to sit up, grimacing at the movement. Fire shot once more through his foot and ankle.

Kathleen took pains to cap the bottle and set it out of his reach. Then she came up beside him, kneeling so she was eye-level with him. "Carson, please don't move. The stinging will stop shortly—"

"*Stinging?* Is that what you call it?" He fell back onto the bed, the effort too much for him to hold himself in a semi-upright position.

She regarded him steadily. "I have been yelled at, cursed at, and called worse names than you can imagine for the last five years of marriage to the 'Reverend' Dill Hyder. I expect better from you, Mr. Ridge."

He swallowed hard. From the way she spoke, he knew she not only expected 'better,' she had been wounded—first by her husband, and now, by him. 'Mr. Ridge' she'd called him. He'd hurt her badly.

He lifted a hand and touched her cheek. "I'm sorry. It—it won't happen again—on my word."

Her hazel eyes held his, and her lips trembled. For a moment, he thought she might break down—and what woman wouldn't? She must be scared, not only for his health, but wondering how she was going to take care of them both in this snowstorm.

She rose from the floor and glanced around the small bedchamber.

"Mr. Maxwell's gone to Texas," she said. "So I've built a fire with the wood he left behind the house, and there was a ham in the smokehouse. I've got it warming."

"The animals?" His voice was a croak as he tried to keep it steady.

Kathleen reached for a tin cup on the nightstand and bent to lift his head.

"I can do it," he muttered, embarrassed at having to have help with the smallest things. He managed to raise himself to a half-sitting position and drank the melted snow. It was like heaven, sliding down cool and smooth, even better than whiskey.

"The horses are in the barn; safe, warm, and with water."

He quirked a brow.

"Your paint was here, just as you predicted," she said. "Looks like when Mr. Maxwell decided to leave, he took what he could carry, but he had to leave some of the meat behind in the smokehouse. That's probably what brought your horse over here. In this weather, that smell would tempt a lot of animals."

"Did you take the gun with you? Outside, I mean. Could have tempted something pretty dangerous."

Kathleen smiled at his concern. "Of course. Who'd take care of you if a pack of wolves got me?"

He gave her an odd look. "I was thinking of you being carried off by them, not what would happen to me if you were." After a moment he asked, "Where's Oscar?"

Kathleen nodded toward the front room. "He's by the fire, getting warmed up."

Carson immediately moved to get up.

"What are you doing?" Kathleen started forward to him, and he grasped her hand.

"Help me, Kath. I want to go in there—with Oscar. This bedroom's cold and...he needs me."

Kathleen nodded. "All right. Let's take it slow. There's a settee in there that's a pretty good size. It's already near the fire—"

They took the first step, a groan escaping Carson's lips. His ankle wasn't broken, but it was badly twisted and swollen, with deep lacerations from the teeth of the trap.

61

It wasn't far to the settee, and they managed to get to it just as Carson was ready to collapse. He let go of Kathleen and sat, none too gracefully, on the dark brown leather.

"Just rest, will you? And let me go stir the beans. Don't move."

He shrugged, looking into her face. "I'm not going anywhere. I may just lie down and sleep again if you promise not to wake me by pouring Maxwell's whiskey over my foot."

She gave a mock sniff. "The way I see it, you should be glad Mr. Maxwell had such a nice stock of liquor he had to leave behind. There are lots of uses for good whiskey."

At that, Carson couldn't hold back his laughter. "And what would you know about 'good whiskey', Kathleen McCain? Oh—I keep forgetting…it's 'Hyder' now, isn't it?" He shifted to put his feet up on the couch, stretching out carefully.

Oscar lay on the floor within petting distance, and he nuzzled Carson's hand.

"Not for much longer," Kathleen stated quietly.

The smile faded. "What do you mean?"

Kathleen turned away from him and started for the kitchen without answering.

"Kathleen, what's going on? Is Dill—*dying*?"

A sharp bark of laughter escaped her as she took up a bowl left behind on the table and wiped it with a clean towel from the pantry.

"No. Nothing so dramatic as that. Though, I'm sure, when all is said and done, he'll wish he *was* dead."

Carson raised a dark brow.

"From the shame of it all," she clarified. "You know, when we're divorced it will be hard for him to keep a congregation. But, he's ashamed of me already, so I think he'll come to see this is for the best." She turned away with the bowl. "I'm going to bring in some snow to melt. Looks like Mr. Maxwell left some tea behind."

"No coffee?"

Kathleen smiled. "I'm certain he had to make a choice. He couldn't carry it all."

"Tea it is, and I'll be grateful for it. Thank you, Kath."

His gaze held hers for a moment. "I wasn't complaining. As long as it's warm, I'm glad to have it."

"I know." She opened the back door and hurried to close it behind her.

***

Carson tried to sort out Kathleen's cryptic responses. It was true, they'd been children together—but that had been a long time ago. And she was younger. Her family had moved when she was nine, and Carson hadn't seen her again until a few months ago.

He and some other Lighthorse officers had joined forces with the posse from Wolf Creek to save Kathleen and her half brother, Derrick, from the remnants of the Davis Gang.

Kathleen had been kidnapped by some of the gang members who had ridden in to Wolf Creek and murdered an innocent woman in the church in their bid to take Kathleen.

No doubt, the preacher, her husband, was worried that she'd been "used" by the outlaws. *Probably hadn't touched her since then*, Carson thought. Reverend Hyder was not one to be overly concerned with others, from what he'd witnessed. Hyder hadn't even joined the posse who'd ridden after her.

Where had she been heading on this cold, snowy day? The day before Christmas Eve…she must've been desperate to get away from Hyder. But why hadn't she gone to Derrick's?

Just then, the door opened, and Kathleen came back inside, pulling it shut behind her. She carried the bowl into the warmth of the main room and set it down beside the fireplace, her fingers red and dripping.

But her cheeks were pink, and there was a light in her eyes that made the hazel color more green. She looked happy, in spite of the fact that she was more than likely going to be spending Christmas snowed in with him, an invalid, in this deserted cabin.

The thought brought a frown to Carson's face.

"I saw a cardinal," Kathleen stated, going to the table to get the towel. "He was sitting right outside on the back gate post. So beautiful, with all the white snow around him." Her voice sounded wistful to Carson, as if she weren't used to beautiful things—or being in a state of mind to ponder them.

"And so free," she went on. She put the towel across her shoulder and stood in front of the fire, warming her hands.

"Where are your gloves?" It was all he could think of to say.

"I didn't want to ruin them," she answered.

"Come here, Kathleen." Carson sat up and held out his hands. "I'll get them warm faster than the fire will."

Gratefully, she came to him and sank to her knees, letting him engulf her frozen hands in his warm ones. She closed her eyes.

"Better?" he asked.

"Oh, yes. This is much quicker."

He grinned. "Now, tell me about the Reverend. And where were you heading all alone on this dreary day? Your husband should be horsewhipped for allowing you out on these roads alone."

"I agree—he *should* be horsewhipped, but that's one of his lesser offenses." She twisted around to sit beside him on the floor, and he pulled part of his blanket around her shoulder. There was an easiness between them, and Carson knew she was about to tell him things she'd never told anyone else.

"I married Dill because I had no other choice. Papa had been murdered, and my older brothers killed in the war. Derrick had left for the war, too, and we didn't know what had become of him. Mama—she and I thought he was gone, too. We had to fend for ourselves. Times were really hard. We had our place, but we didn't have any money."

Carson nodded. He knew the ravages that war could bring, not only to the whites but also to his people, the Cherokee. Two women alone…

"Dill asked me to marry him. I accepted, but…I didn't love him." She looked down at where her fingers entwined beneath the edge of the blanket.

"He blamed me for being barren."

"How did he know *he* wasn't at fault?"

65

Kathleen laughed softly. "Dill has never been wrong or to blame for anything in his life. He's ten years older than I am, you know."

Carson grinned. "You have issues with us older men?" She turned to look at him, her seriousness making him sorry he'd tried to joke with her.

"Carson, please…don't ever lump yourself in a group with Dill Hyder."

The vehemence in her tone drew him up short. *What in the hell had Dill Hyder done to her?*

Carson put a hand out to touch her cheek. Kathleen was beautiful, the way she looked at him now. Beseeching him not to compare himself with Dill…*ever*. It had been a joke, but she didn't see it that way.

"Talk to me." His voice came out hoarse and ragged. He could only hope she'd think it due to his injury rather than the burgeoning anger that swelled inside him at Dill's mistreatment of her. *She was not his to protect.*

"It's shameful," she whispered, glancing away from him. "After we married, he began to treat me as his property. I always knew ours was not a love match. Dill wanted children—I did, too. But I was never able to—to conceive."

Carson remained impassive, waiting for her to continue.

"He always picked at me about my unseemly behavior—a look, a smile—a word I should not have spoken—" She broke off. "I don't know how he ever thought I'd make a good mother. I couldn't please him as a wife."

"Some people can't be satisfied, Kath. No matter how we try."

She gave him a quick smile. "That's kind of you, Carson."

"Did he ever become...physical?"

She shook her head, hesitantly. "Not—Not recently." At his black look, she rushed on. "But *I* did."

"How so?"

"We argued. I told him I was going to a friend's for Christmas. He forbade me to go. Then he said I...couldn't be trusted." Her voice fell to a whisper. "After I was kidnapped, he said he didn't know what I 'let' them do. That he could never have...relations with me again, now that I had been with—so many men."

Carson felt the anger boiling through him, overtaking the pain of his injured foot. He tried to keep from moving, but she must have felt the tension ripple through his arm lying against the back of her neck.

She didn't look at him. "I—just couldn't stand any more of his—his insults. I—"

"Kath? What?" Carson shifted on the sofa and put his arm around her. She laid her head against him as she turned, and he could see tears in her leashes.

"I hit him, Carson. I—"

Carson tried not to smile at the thought of the pompous ass getting a good old-fashioned much overdue slap across his face. "Many women have slapped their husbands at some time—"

"You don't understand. I didn't just *slap* him. I punched him with my fist. I gave him a black eye."

Carson pulled her into his arms awkwardly, because of their positions—him on the sofa, her on the floor beside him. He knew Kathleen. He didn't dare say or do what he wanted. How he would have loved to have congratulated her for a punch well-landed!

Instead, he held her for a moment before he spoke. "Do you believe he deserved it?"

"Yes," she answered quickly. "Oh, yes. If I'd been a man I wouldn't have stopped at one." She fell silent, then softly said, "But if I'd been a man, he would never have talked to me like he did in the first place."

"Why didn't you just go to Derrick's?"

She gave him a wry look, but didn't move her head from where it rested against his chest. "Derrick would have killed him for the things he said."

Carson nodded. "I may help him do just that when this foot heals."

Kathleen's lips quirked. "You all won't have a chance. He'll die of shame before you can get to him. Sporting a black eye—and with no believable explanation other than what happened. How will he face his congregation? Or the people of Wolf Creek? Then, with me leaving like I did—another shame. Everyone will know I gave him that shiner."

"That he deserved," Carson added.

"Even so—" She sighed. "I can't bring myself to regret it, even though I probably should."

"Kath—" Carson's mind was so full of all the things he wanted to say, he didn't know where to start. He wanted to comfort her, but he also was suddenly uncertain of his own feelings. When she'd described Dill's treatment of her, Carson had realized the white-hot anger that flooded him was not the normal intensity he might have felt for just any woman. Ever since he'd seen her, when he'd helped rescue her and Derrick from the outlaw camp, something had nagged at him.

Now, he was beginning to understand. He cared more for Kathleen than maybe he should. She was married. He would never bring disgrace to her.

She was close to him now, her head nestled against him. Closer than was proper. The fire warmed them, and coupled with the smell of the beans in the pot, Carson was reminded of the home he'd had as a child. The hollow feeling he'd carried so long in his chest began to dissipate, to be replaced with a contentment he'd never known. But he knew he couldn't get used to it. When they were able, they'd leave here, and Kathleen...would most likely go back to Dill. She'd have time to think, and she'd probably talk herself into believing she'd somehow done something wrong.

"What are you planning to do? When we're able to leave, I mean?"

Kathleen raised her head and looked at him. "I don't know. I only know I will never live as Dill Hyder's wife again, nor under the same roof with him, for even one night." Her voice shook.

"What about going to Briartown, with your mother?" He didn't say what lay unspoken between them, but Kathleen did.

"No. She and your father deserve their time alone right now, after all these years of being separated. With Derrick and Leah just married, I don't want to be a burden to them, either."

Carson didn't voice it, and he wondered if she'd thought of it yet, but if the town of Wolf Creek ever realized she'd spent the night in a secluded, snowed-in cabin with him, she'd be painted in the exact light that Dill already thought of her. And being the woman of an Indian was thought of, in some parts, as worse than supposedly being used by several of the outlaws in the remnants of Clark Davis's gang.

That had never happened, though, according to Derrick and Kathleen. But Dill Hyder, damn his smarmy, vicious soul, would make it seem that way to turn it to his advantage; to make Kathleen the wrong-doer.

"What about keeping your home and giving him the boot?"

She shook her head. "I don't think I can bear it, Carson. That house—I'd looked forward to a home of my own, a family…but it didn't ever come about. Now—to go back there where there were so many unhappy memories made—I can't." She looked around the cabin.

"You see—this place already feels like more of a home to me than the house where Dill and I lived. Why, I've a mind to slog out to the barn and see if I can find an ax. There's a little pine tree, just yonder." She pointed toward the back door. "I think I'll cut it and bring it inside. We'll have ourselves a Christmas tree!"

Carson smiled at her enthusiasm. "Don't be out there long," he warned softly. His fingers trailed through her hair as she started to get up. She met his gaze questioningly, but he veiled his expression. "You're too dear to me to lose you to pneumonia."

She shook her head. "Only for a few more days until you can get around on your own. I'm really not dear to anyone, Carson. Certainly not my husband."

***

Kathleen trudged through the snowdrifts to the barn. She wanted to check on the animals, but she needed to get away from the intensity in Carson's deep gaze. If she wasn't careful, he'd be able to tell. Her hand trembled on the barn door handle. She tried to convince herself he was only being kind to her. She couldn't misread kindness for a different kind of caring. The only thing that could worsen her situation was to be made another kind of fool. She had behaved with total impropriety already, leaning against him as she had. They were childhood friends—nothing more.

She silently berated herself as she swung the barn door open and walked toward the animals. After making sure their water wasn't frozen, and seeing that they'd eaten the oats she'd put out for them, she began her search for a hatchet or an ax. The tree she had her eye on was small. *Perfect.*

Mr. Maxwell had not taken tools with him. Luckily for her, he'd left most everything behind. A small hatchet hung on the wall, and she quickly lifted it from its resting place and carried it outside.

She headed straight for the little tree and brushed the snow away from the bottom, then began to swing the ax. It wouldn't take long. She was already looking forward to decorating it, but she couldn't imagine how. Maybe that was what made this such a grand adventure—everything was an unknown…especially Carson Ridge.

***

There was another place for Kathleen to get away from the mess she was in with Dill, Carson thought. One he'd carefully refrained from mentioning—because he wasn't sure of what she'd think.

And he wasn't certain of his own feelings toward her, either. But it was all becoming clearer to him by the second.

When he remembered how they'd found Derrick and Kathleen at Demon's Drop, his stomach flipped over. Watching Clark Davis's band of outlaws torture his half-brother, even for the briefest moment until the posse could get fully into position, had been the hardest thing Carson had ever had to do. He and Derrick had both inherited their Cherokee stoicism from the father they shared, Collin Ridge.

But, he had to admit, it had brought red-hot heat rushing through his body when he'd seen Kathleen—her hands tied, clothing dirty and torn, her blonde hair a glorious mess—with defiance still flashing in her eyes despite everything she'd been through.

Though Kathleen was no blood kin to him, Carson had always felt responsibility for her in their growing up years—she and Derrick shared a mother; he and Derrick shared a father; Derrick was not only Carson's best friend, he was blood. Kathleen and Derrick were blood, but none that Carson shared, since it was through their mother. Still, Carson had always taken special care to watch out for Kathleen. He'd failed her. His fists clenched as he thought of what he'd love to do to that sorry son of a bitch she was married to.

Which brought him back to his earlier musings. *Where would she go?*

She'd said she felt at home here. From the looks of the cabin, Mr. Maxwell did not intend to return. The cryptic note he'd left verified it…and it was a good, safe place.

A perfect place to heal a mangled foot, and a broken heart.

Kathleen's life had been rough. Her father, Andrew McCain, had uprooted the family from Briartown all those years past when he'd realized his wife, Fiona, had betrayed him with Collin Ridge. He'd moved from Indian Territory to Kansas in the hopes of starting over.

But Fiona's heart had stayed behind with Carson and Derrick's father, Collin Ridge.

Kathleen had married Dill Hyder out of necessity, not love. It had been a disaster in the making.

The door opened and Kathleen stomped the snow off as best she could, then turned to drag the small tree inside.

Carson started up off the sofa, but the pain in his twisted ankle brought him up short. He eased himself back down with a grimace, glad Kathleen had her back turned.

"Look, Carson! Isn't it perfect?" She gave him a wide grin as she pulled the tree into the front room where he sat.

The dog lifted his head from his paws, then rested easy again when he realized there was no threat.

"There's a bucket in the barn. I'm going to bring it in and stack some short pieces of firewood in it to hold the tree in place."

Carson looked at her doubtfully.

"It's all we've got. And it'll do—just as long as we have a tree."

He gave her a faint smile, and she laughed at his expression. "Oh, I know I'm being a silly goose. But I'm excited."

"And happy."

She nodded. "What an adventure this is!"

Carson shook his head. "Tongues will wag, for sure, Kath. You...me...together overnight."

"Or maybe for days," she added wickedly. "Why, there's no telling what we might do!"

"Raid the pantry?" he suggested.

"Use up all the firewood—how decadent!"

"Sleep under the same roof—with no chaperone..." Carson's eyes glimmered with laughter.

"Sir, you forget yourself! I'm a married woman, you know," she teased, then became serious. "But, not for long. Especially after this. If Dill thought I'd been defiled by the Davis Gang, there's no end to what he'll imagine happening between you and me." She'd managed to get the tree propped in the corner by the fireplace. Turning toward Carson once more, she tried to meet his eyes, but couldn't.

"You know—" he started.

She waved him off. "Of course. I know you'd never be improper."

"I was going to say, 'You know, it doesn't have to be left to Dill Hyder's imagination.'"

She gave him a startled look, but he didn't smile. He wasn't teasing anymore. He held his hand out to her, and she closed the small space between them, taking his warm fingers in hers.

He pulled her to him and put his mouth to hers in a thorough kiss that made her tremble with anticipation.

"Kath…" he muttered close to her mouth. "You should know me better. I *would* be improper. *Highly…*"

She put her hand to his cheek, kneeling beside him on the floor. The fire was warming, but not nearly as much as Carson's kiss. It was like nothing she'd ever known. *But she'd dreamed of it. Plenty of nights she'd lain awake, wishing her life could be different—and not just since the abduction.*

"Carson—" She drew back slowly. His obsidian eyes burned with an inner fire. With a start, she realized she was looking at desire—naked and pure—his want for her.

She was certain he saw the same, reflected in her own eyes. And as much as she hated to leave the shelter of his arms, she could not betray her wedding vows. She had too much honor for that, despite what her husband thought—at least until she was able to tell him that their marriage was dissolved.

"If you are expecting an apology," he murmured, "it's not coming."

She shook her head, flustered. "No. I was expecting a lightning bolt," she answered.

He deliberately misunderstood. "What? I must be doing something wrong if you didn't feel it—I sure as hell did."

He pulled her to him again, and she came with no resistance, easily fitting herself into his arms once more.

Her heart pounded as their lips met again, and when the kiss ended, it left her as breathless as the one before it.

Carson's dark eyes were veiled, but he relaxed back onto the sofa with a low sigh, moistening his lips as if to savor the taste of her.

"Carson—we can't. I'm married, remember?"

A sardonic laugh escaped him. "If you can call it that."

Kathleen looked away. "I said my vows. Once Dill and I are...divorced—"

"Kathleen—have you ever thought that Dill might not let that happen?"

She shook her head "I will leave him. I will not live with him. I'll stay right here if I have to." She looked around the little cabin. The fire burned cheerily, Oscar lying nearby with his bandaged paw. The beans bubbled on the stove, sending out an aroma that made her stomach twinge. The furnishings were sparse and well-used, but serviceable. And the little tree stood, still waiting for her to set it to rights, but the scent of pine already filled the warmth of the room. It smelled like home. It felt like home. And Kathleen had to admit that a big part of that was the comfortable companionship she shared with Carson Ridge.

Carson's even stare brought her thoughts back to what she'd been saying about staying here. Why not? It was highly unlikely Mr. Maxwell was ever going to return.

"I don't mind living here alone," she said, raising her chin a notch. "I've been alone, really, the past few years, anyhow."

Carson reached out and touched her hair. "Kathleen, it's liable to get rough when you and Dill make your final break. I'm here. I'll stand by you, and—God help him if he raises a hand to you."

"He's tried that before," she said ruefully. "No. I'm done with Dill…with his accusations and his constant preaching and condemnation of everyone and everything. There's no room in his heart for me or a love of anything but himself. I'm not afraid of him, Carson. But…I do appreciate your offer."

Reluctantly, Kathleen rose from the floor, leaving the warmth and acceptance of Carson's touch.

"I'll go—"

"Shh—listen." Carson sat up and put his fingers around her wrist to keep her from moving. He cocked his head. "Riders."

Kathleen hurried away from him to look out the window. In the gray of the late afternoon, she could make out four men, riding up the trail to the front door.

"Kath?"

She breathed a sigh of relief. "It's Derrick," she said. But her breathing all but gave out as she realized who was with him.

"What's wrong?"

She turned from the window to look at Carson. "Remember the lightning bolt I mentioned?"

A slow smile came across Carson's lips. "I thought we remedied that."

She shook her head. "The other kind. The kind that hits you when you've done something wrong."

"Ah. He brought Dill with him," Carson said mildly.

Kathleen nodded. "And the marshal, along with his deputy."

Carson grimaced as he sat up. "Gardner? He doesn't have jurisdiction out here. Do me a favor, will you, Kath? Bring me my guns."

***

"Kathleen! Open this door!" Dill raged as soon as he'd slid down from the saddle.

"Better be obedient one last time," Carson said wryly. "I want to get a look at this shiner you gave him."

Kathleen shook her head, then pulled the door open. "Goodness," she fussed. "You all come in out of the cold."

From the fireplace, Oscar lifted his head and gave a soft growl.

"Just wait," Carson murmured, giving him a quick look.

Dill was first through the door. His face was mottled with cold and anger. But when he looked down the barrel of Carson's Henry, all the color drained and fear replaced everything else. Before he could say anything, Marshal Gardner and Deputy Quint Croy stepped through the door, followed by Derrick.

"Well, now lookie here," Gardner said with a questioning smile. He took off his hat and started for the fire. Oscar growled once more, and Carson spoke to him in Cherokee. Gardner had stopped mid-stride at the warning from the wolf-dog, but now he stood in front of the fireplace, warming his backside.

Derrick spoke to the marshal, but never took his angry gaze from Dill. "This is Carson Ridge, Sam, of the Cherokee Light-horse."

"Carson." The marshal nodded in greeting, then looked at Kathleen. "And Miss Kathleen."

"I knew it!" Dill exploded, his earlier trepidation forgotten with both lawmen there, even though Carson still aimed a gun at him. "Whorin' around again! I might have figured you were up to something. Everything's been different since you were kidnapped. I sometimes wonder if you didn't have that arranged."

Kathleen stood staring at him, speechless in her anger and disbelief.

"You better shut that kind of talk up, Hyder, or I'll make that shiner Kathleen gave you the least of your worries," Derrick said, taking a step toward Dill.

Quint put out a staying hand, silently stopping Derrick's advance.

"I can tell you, Hyder, your wife has certainly not been 'whoring around', as you so delicately put it. I'm the only man here, and I can vouch for the fact there's been no *whoring* going on," Carson said dryly. "I was on my way to your house for Christmas, Derrick, when that fool dog sprung a trap while he was roaming ahead of me. I got down to free him and—there was another one, under the snow.

"Mrs. Hyder came upon me and helped free my foot. We took shelter here from the weather."

Dill gave a loud snort. *"Arranged meeting,* I'm thinking. Let's see that foot of yours that's supposedly injured."

Carson brought the rifle to bear on Dill's chest. "You believe in everything being 'arranged', Hyder? I can *arrange* your permanent six-foot underground home. Keep your distance, Preacher." He nodded toward his foot. "I hear wounds can get infected from *dirt*."

Dill stopped short, his face twisting in disgust.

Marshal Gardner cleared his throat. "Well, let's get down to business as to why we're here. Christmas Eve bein' tomorrow, I'm sure we're all needing to get back to our homes." He turned to Kathleen. "The Reverend says you—uh—cold cocked him a couple of days back. That true?"

Kathleen smiled. "Well, Marshal, *someone* gave him that black eye. And yes, I'm proud to say it was me."

"Jezebel," Dill muttered.

"He's prepared to press charges with Sheriff Satterlee for assault," Gardner said.

"The hell you say!" Carson started up from his seat.

"Well…" Kathleen looked at the marshal, then turned her gaze directly upon Dill. "I'm afraid, Marshal, that—should that happen—I will have to press some charges of my own."

Dill's head jerked up, his eyes locking with hers. The room fell silent.

"Uh…okay, Mrs. Hyder." Marshal Gardner stepped away from the fire. His expression remained neutral, but Kathleen could see he was uncomfortable with the turn their visit was taking.

"What were you—thinking those charges might be?"

"Oh, Marshal, I'm not *thinking*. I was *there*. The night after Derrick and I were rescued from the Davis Gang, my dear husband became—shall we say—*violently* upset with me. He called me a whore. He expressed the belief that I had—given myself to many members of the gang willingly. He slapped me, numerous times—"

"Mrs. Hyder!" Dill shouted, starting for her.

Quint put himself in front of Hyder menacingly. "No, you don't, Reverend."

"—and jerked my hair, put bruises on my arms and—"

"I order you to be quiet! For the love of God, as your husband, I order—"

"You are *not* my husband! Not any longer! Not after the things you've said and done! *You are a monster!*"

The room fell silent as Kathleen's voice vibrated , then faded.

"Kinda tend to agree…if what your wife says is true, Hyder," Gardner said after a moment. "Is it?" He took a step toward Dill. "Look at me, Hyder. Is it true?"

Dill slowly raised his head to meet Gardner's steady gaze. He nodded. "Yes…yes, but she *deserved* it, after what she did! Lying with those—those *animals*—just to save *him*!" He shot a glare at Derrick, who stood nearby, relaxed, his expression neutral.

"Damn savage! He was a part of that gang—they'd never have killed him. I know Kathleen didn't have to do what she did. She must have enjoyed the carnal sins she engaged in. Yet," he lifted his head, posing nobly, "I would take her back to avoid…talk. Now," he glared at Carson, "I shall most likely be forced to proceed with my earlier purpose. It's obvious that my adulterous wife has sinned against God once more, with this…" his lips turned downward in distaste as he nodded toward Carson, "…this *savage.*"

Neither Gardner nor Croy was quick enough to catch Derrick before his hand shot out, spinning Hyder to face him. He jerked the Reverend close to him.

"You son of a bitch." Derrick's hand tightened around Hyder's shirt front beneath his unbuttoned coat. "You keep your filthy mouth shut, *Preacher*, else you'll have a match for the right side. And believe me, I can hit a helluva lot harder than my sister can. You ever lay a hand on her again, you'll find out."

"He—He's threatening me, Marshal!" Hyder's voice rose an octave in his fear.

Gardner smiled, but it never reached his eyes. "I can't say as I blame him, Hyder. I don't cotton to a man slandering a woman—or beating one." His expression hardened. "In fact, I despise it. I think you best forget your so-called charges and head on back home. Now that we know Mrs. Hyder is *safe*, I expect she'll come on home— or not—when she takes a notion."

"What goes on between a man and his wife is no business of the law, Marshal, you have no right to interfere."

"You were begging me to interfere all the way out here. Besides, as I told you, Deputy Croy and I have no jurisdiction outside Wolf Creek—this is Sheriff Satterlee's territory. Quint and I are just here to keep you from doing something *else* you might regret, Preacher. Keepin' the peace, you might say. And when I'm outside my jurisdiction, on my own time, I have a damned short fuse with wife-beaters."

Derrick slowly eased his grip and pushed Hyder away from him. His dark eyes bored into Hyder unmercifully.

Quint nodded at Kathleen. "Ma'am. Are you in need of anything?"

"No, thank you, Deputy." Kathleen smiled.

"Horses fed and watered?" Derrick asked, glancing at Carson.

"Kathleen did it. She's been busy," Carson added to needle Dill. "Took care of the horses and Oscar, here. Put beans on for dinner. Took care of my ankle...even chopped us a Christmas tree."

"Damn it, Kathleen!" Dill turned to her, his face mottled an unflattering red and white in his rage. "You all are witnesses to my wife's infidelity."

"I haven't seen her do anything but show the Christmas spirit, Preacher. The *Christian* spirit," Gardner said. "I'm put in the mind of the story of the Good Samaritan." He pinned Hyder with a stare. "You know that one, don't you, Reverend? Now, I suggest we head on back to Wolf Creek before darkness falls."

Hyder drew himself up. "Without my *wife*, sir? Surely, you cannot be serious, Marshal!"

Gardner shrugged. "Don't believe she's inclined to accompany you."

"Well—well *force* her!"

"*Kidnap* her, you mean?" Gardner asked blandly. "Like the Davis Gang did?"

"Over my dead body—*and yours*." Carson's steady words were a promise as he shot Hyder a glare.

"He threatened me, too!" Hyder jabbed a finger at Carson.

"It's more than a threat, you sorry piece of shit, it's a promise!" Carson roared. He started to his feet, but Kathleen made a sound in her throat and rushed to him.

"No." She put her hands on his arm, bringing the rifle he held down to point at the floor. She sank to her knees beside him, her expression beseeching him to do no violence. "Don't, Carson. He's not that important—not to me, not to...*us*."

Carson turned slowly to look at her.

"Just—let him go. He's not part of my life anymore."

"I'm your husband! Damn you, Mrs. Hyder, you are my wife!"

Kathleen finally tore her gaze away from Carson to look at Dill. "Not anymore, Dill. I'm divorcing you."

"D-Divorcing me? You'll ruin me! I can't preach anymore if I'm divorced. How will I live? How will I face the townsfolk of Wolf Creek?"

"Maybe you ought to think about moving on, Hyder," Derrick said. "Find another town to settle in where they don't know you."

"I most certainly will not!"

Derrick moved close to him again. "I'm just sayin' ...might be a good idea for you...*wife beater* that you are, and all that. I better not run into you in a dark alley, you bastard. And if you know what's good for you, you'll speak kindly—*very kindly*—of my sister to anyone who asks. In other words, this split up is due to your own personal problems—and God knows, you've got plenty of 'em—and you can only hope Kathleen finds it in her heart to forgive you."

"Well, Miss Kathleen, we'll be going now, I reckon, if all is well," Gardner broke in jovially. "I'll ask Doctor Munro to make a trip out here first thing tomorrow morning to have a look at your injury, Carson."

"Thanks, Marshal."

Gardner and Croy started for the door. The marshal opened it, and Quint stood aside to let Hyder pass.

"Let's go, Preacher," Quint said when Hyder dawdled.

"Kathleen, you have not seen the last of me," Hyder said proudly. "I will not let you go easily."

"Oh, Dill." Kathleen shook her head. "You are out of my life. Completely."

"You won't receive anything from me. Not one penny. Nothing."

Kathleen rose and took a step toward Dill, so she could look him directly in the face. "What I wanted most from you, I already have. *Your absence from my world.*"

Gardner tipped his hat in silent salute as he went through the door. Dill started to reply, but Quint took him by the arm and hustled him out the door.

"Evenin'," Quint said with a nod to Kathleen, closing the door firmly behind him.

"Kathleen? You sure you're okay stayin' here? We're in for more snow, I'm thinkin'," Derrick stood uncertainly beside the door.

"We'll be fine, especially if Doc Munro comes out in the morning." She glanced at Carson. "Your brother's in no shape to travel, anyhow."

Derrick nodded, glancing toward Carson.

"Oh—uh—yeah, I couldn't travel. I've had a fever and my leg throbs to even think of getting up."

"Didn't throb a minute ago when you were goin' after Hyder."

"Would you like to eat dinner with us?" Kathleen put in quickly.

But Derrick shook his head. "No, Leah will have supper ready time I get home." He nodded toward Carson. "Maybe you'll feel well enough by Christmas Day to ride on out to the house."

Carson looked doubtful, and Derrick had to hide a smile. "If not, I'll make a run out here with some food."

"We'll be fine," Kathleen insisted.

"What're you gonna do with that tree?" Derrick nodded toward the tree Kathleen had brought in earlier.

"I chopped it, and I was planning to set it up in a bucket from out in the barn. I guess I better—"

"I'll do it," Derrick said gruffly. "I've already done one of these today."

"You? You and Leah have your first Christmas tree? That's really—uh—sweet," Carson finished, ending his teasing at Derrick's glowering look.

"What do you call this?" Derrick crossed the room and picked up the tree. "Somebody *else* is having their first Christmas tree together, aren't they?" His look moved slowly from Carson to Kathleen.

"I'll go stir the beans." Kathleen headed for the kitchen.

"What the hell's going on here, Carson?" Derrick asked in a low voice. "I never saw this coming."

"Me, either," Carson admitted. "But you have no worries. My intentions are completely honorable."

Derrick gave a short laugh, and Carson gave him an innocent look. "Kathleen's a grown woman, Derrick. What are you worried about?"

"She's headstrong. And not always for her own good."

Carson gave him a faint smile. "You saying I'm not *'for her own good'*?"

"I'll go get this taken care of," Derrick muttered, heading for the door.

When he was gone, Kathleen came back to the front room to sit on the floor in front of Carson.

"I'm starved," she admitted, though it was unladylike, she knew.

Carson chuckled. "You worked up an appetite tellin' Dill where the cow ate the cabbage. Feel better?"

"I'm just relieved it's over."

"It's not, though, Kath," he said quietly. "You're not divorced yet."

At his somber tone, Kathleen turned around to look at hm. "It doesn't matter, Carson. In my mind, Dill and I are no more. We haven't been for…a long time, if we ever were. I'm ready to start fresh." She paused and took a deep breath. "I'm glad you were here with me. I should have left him a long time ago."

Derrick had called her 'headstrong', Carson thought. And though she was determined, he could understand how leaving a man like Dill might be a frightening thing. Dill Hyder was a so-called man of God, but Carson knew better. Dill was a coward and a bully who hid behind his godliness. Kathleen was going to need all the support she could find in Wolf Creek once Dill's vindictive streak showed itself. But now, it was a time for celebration, and for happiness.

He smiled at her. "Well, you got your Christmas wish. A home for Christmas."

Kathleen looked around the little cabin, love in her eyes. "Yes, it really is a home; the home I always imagined," she said softly.

Carson nodded. It was too soon to tell what the future might hold, but miracles weren't impossible. It was Christmas, after all…a time when dreams could come true, according to legend… even here in Wolf Creek.

THE END

THE ANGEL TREE

Chuck Tyrell

Brandy was lucky. She knew she was lucky. Just being at Miss Abby's was lucky.

Most of the men who came to Miss Abby's house were on their best manners. If they weren't, Miss Abby never let them in the front door again.

Brandy got hit once. Cecil Cranz hit her hard. Right in the face. Gave her a black eye and a good-sized bruise on her cheekbone. Naturally, she screeched. She scampered around the bed so Cecil couldn't get his hands on her again. He couldn't move well, his pants down around his ankles and all.

Howie Perkins came busting into Brandy's room. Miss Abby didn't allow the rooms to be locked. He carried an oak truncheon and knew just how to use it. In a second, he was back of Cecil with the truncheon across Cecil's neck and up under his chin. Cecil couldn't do a thing but gurgle.

"You went and hurt Miss Brandy," Howie said, in a little boy voice that didn't match his big body and hard muscles. "You'll have to leave now, and you're not welcome to ever come back. Now I'll give you enough slack that you can pull up your pants, but you gotta carry your boots downstairs in your own hands."

Downstairs, Miss Abby told Cecil there would be no charge—she always did that—and told him again that he would never be welcome at any establishment she had any interest in—establishment was the word she always used.

Brandy's black eye and bruised cheek kept her out of work for nearly two weeks, because Miss Abby said she did not want Brandy's condition giving customers any wayward ideas. Those two weeks were when Brandy learned what it was like in the cribs.

The first day, she hurt too much to think of anything other than bathing her eye and cheek with cool wet washcloths. That was after Miss Abby made her hold a thick slice of raw beefsteak against where Cecil had hit her. The next day, though her cheek was still sore and her eye was swollen, Brandy had to get out. Sitting in the kitchen or in her room doing nothing bored her silly.

Brandy had some regular clothes. While she was at Miss Abby's, she didn't need all that many. Strange, but most of the men who came to see her didn't even make her get undressed. Of course, she never wore bustles. They just got in the way.

She shrugged a calico dress over her head and shoved her arms into its long sleeves. It hung like a sack from her shoulders, but she decided that might be an advantage. And, it being December, she pulled on wool leggings she'd knitted herself and donned her warmest coat, which was not all that warm because she rarely left Miss Abby's snug house.

She pulled a bonnet low over her face. The wool muffler she borrowed from Annabelle came up to her nose. She looked in the mirror—Miss Abby insisted that each girl have a mirror. "Learn how to make yourself look like a lady," she said. "Use the mirror. It shows you what other people see." Brandy saw two bright blue eyes, one a little bloodshot, and a lot of clothing. Maybe people wouldn't notice the bruises.

Brandy went downstairs to Miss Abby's room. Raising a hesitant hand, she knocked, almost without making a sound. Of course, no one answered. She rapped harder.

"Who is it?"

"It's me, ma'am, Brandy."

"What do you want, dear?"

"May I go for a walk?"

"It's awfully cold outside."

"I know. But I'd truly like to get some fresh air."

"As you wish, dear. Please stay south of Useless Street, and don't be gone too long, do you hear?"

"Yes, ma'am. Thank you, ma'am."

Brandy let herself out of the back door. She remembered to bring a few coins from her hoard. Miss Abby kept most of her earnings, "in trust," she said. Miss Abby always talked of Evangeline when she spoke of money. "Remember how it was when Evangeline married Tom Briggins? On that occasion, I was able to give her the money I'd held in trust. More than a hundred dollars, it was."

Brandy wasn't sure if it was all in her favor. After all, every customer paid Miss Abby five dollars, and new customers paid in advance. Brandy wasn't all that good at math, but she knew that twenty pokes would work out to a hundred dollars, and she had at least twenty customers a month, and a lot more when the herds were in.

So Miss Abby kept Brandy's share of what the customers paid, but Brandy kept the little gratuities they left for her. A few half-dimes. A cartwheel. It all added up.

The cold slapped her nearly as hard as Cecil's callused hand. She slipped her hands beneath her arms. She didn't have a hand muff. Perhaps she should buy herself one for Christmas and say it came from Saint Nicholas. Not that any of the women at Miss Abby's would believe her. The cold bit at her nose.

Out back of Miss Abby's, Wolf Creek rippled along its way toward the Arkansas. Brandy walked a few steps to the back fence, opened the gate, and stepped around to Useless Street. She took the south side of the road past the Wolf's Den. Horses, shaggy in their winter coats, stood at the hitching rail, white clouds forming around their noses in the cold air. One spread his rear legs, hunched a little, and sent a steaming stream of urine splashing and splatting on the hard ground. Brandy smiled a tiny smile to herself. To think, some men believed themselves well endowed.

Past the rickety stores with doors open in hopes for business on the south side of Useless, Brandy wended her way through tent city to the banks of Wolf Creek again. Trickles of sewage ran down depressions in the banks of the creek, but grassy humps offered ample space to sit, even though the grass was brown in December. Sandpipers and plovers hunted amongst the dried grass where the water was shallow. A darter swam by, only a long neck and a head with a beak as sharp as a darning needle showing above the water. Soon it would snow. It always snowed before Christmas. But now, Brandy could sit on the grass left over from summer and breathe in the crisp air on the breeze that wafted from across Wolf Creek.

The sound of children's laughter came from further downstream. Surely they were not playing in the water, not on a day as cold as this. Brandy stood up, brushed the dry grass from the back of her dress, and ambled downstream to find out what made the children laugh.

Brandy walked slowly because she didn't want to startle the children by coming up on them all of a sudden. She knew that sometimes kids didn't want grown-ups to know what they were doing. After all, she'd been a kid not all that long ago. She pushed through a stand of willows to where she could see what the children were doing. They'd gathered in a small clearing amongst the willows on the north bank of Wolf Creek. They'd been there before. Brandy could tell because of the pathway trampled around a small boxwood tree that grew in the middle of the clearing. The children laughed with joy as they danced around the little tree, as if they'd forgotten the holes in the elbows of their raggedy coats and the patches on their trousers. Even the little girls wore trousers.

Brandy pushed on into the clearing. "Hi," she said. "Shouldn't you all be in school?"

At the sound of her voice, all four children stopped short. All four faces whipped around to stare at Brandy. All four breathed white clouds out of open mouths into the crisp air. But there could never have been so different a four as those: a tall boy with kinky hair and coffee skin; a girl with huge brown eyes, straight black hair, and skin of ivory; a younger, red-haired boy with a face covered with freckles; and a tiny China doll with golden hair peeking from a worn knit cap and huge blue eyes that seem to take up half her red-cheeked smiling face.

"Who're you?" the biggest boy said.

"Brandy."

"Funny name."

"Whatcha doing?" Brandy asked.

"None a' your damn business."

Brandy shrugged. "Shouldn't you be in school?" she said again.

The boy ducked his curly head and dug at the dried grass with the toe of his worn-out shoe. "Can't," he said. He didn't sound happy about it either.

"Why not?"

The boy said nothing.

The bigger girl spoke up. "Miss Brandy. You know that everyone in town don't want kids from across Useless Street at their school. Know what they call us? They call us 'bastards'. You know what else? They say bastards like us ain't welcome at the school or anywhere else, that's what they say."

"Who smacked you?" the red-haired boy said.

"What makes you think someone smacked me? Maybe I ran into a door or something."

"Ma gets smacked. An' when it happens, she looks like you look. Your belly black and blue?"

"My belly?"

"Yeah. You been smacked so I figured maybe you got kicked too. Ma gets kicked sometimes."

Brandy changed the subject. "What's that on the boxwood tree?"

"Decorations," the girl said. "Christmas soon, so we decorated our Angel Tree."

"Looks like a boxwood tree to me," Brandy said. "Why do you call it an Angel Tree?"

The children looked at each other like the Angel Tree was their own secret and they didn't want to share it with anyone.

Brandy knelt on the dried grass of the clearing so she'd be at the same eye level as the children. "Why don't you tell me your names? I told you mine."

The tall boy said, "I'm Brad. I mean Braddock. Yeah, Braddock, but ever'one calls me Brad, or boy, or shitface. Or nothing."

The dark girl said, "I'm Juanita. Sometimes people call me kid, or greaser brat, or just girl. But mostly they pretend I'm not there."

The other boy said, "Ted's my name. But Ma calls me Teddy."

And the littlest girl, who was probably no more than four years old, said, "Maddy. That's who I is. Really."

"I'm so pleased to meet you all at the Angel Tree," Brandy said. "I don't have many friends. Would you be my friends?"

"Why?" Brad asked. Brad was biggest and seemed to be the leader.

"I really would like some friends, being as I don't have more than one or two. Four fine friends like you would make me very happy."

The four children walked away from Brandy, almost halfway across the clearing, then put their arms around each other's shoulders and their heads together. Brad did most of the talking, but Brandy couldn't hear what he said.

She sat back on the brown grass with her arms around her knees. Little white clouds, quite puffy for wintertime, nearly covered the sky. Maybe angels breathed them there. The breeze switched and came from the north, colder now. Brandy hugged herself against the cold. The children didn't seem to notice.

The Angel Tree stood silent in the middle of the clearing. Brandy wondered if it knew any secrets. The children had tied bits of bright yarn and pieces of cloth to the branches. Because it would soon be Christmas, they said.

The children broke their huddle and marched over to stand in front of Brandy, tallest on her right, tiny Maddy at the left. Brad spoke. "You can be our friend, but you have to promise."

"Promise what?"

"The Angel Tree is a secret. You have to promise to keep it a secret. You have to keep this whole place secret. Do you promise?"

"I promise."

"Cross your heart and hope to die if you break your promise?"

Brandy drew an X over her heart and repeated, "Cross my heart and hope to die if I ever break my promise."

Brad nodded. "Good," he said. "Now, spit in your right hand."

Brandy did.

Brad spit in his hand and offered it to Brandy to shake. She took his hand. "Friends forever," she said.

"Forever," Brad said.

Brandy repeated the ritual with each child. Now she was bound to them and they to her. Friends forever.

"I'm your forever friend, so you can tell me about the Angel Tree, can't you?" Brandy said. They all sat on the uphill side of the tree. The children unconsciously copied Brandy, putting their arms around their knees as she did.

Then Juanita began to sing. "Come gather round the Angel Tree, come warm a heart and fill a need." The other children joined her, singing softly in bell-clear tones. "Not just once, but the whole year through, see what a gift of love can do."

Brandy realized they were watching her face as they sang. "Come gather round the Angel Tree, twinkling lights for all to see." She couldn't help smiling at the angelic expressions on their faces. "Angels beckon us with pleading tones to bring God's plenty to every home."

"The Angel Tree, the Angel Tree, our very own, each good deed sown, come gather round the Angel Tree."

"What a lovely song," Brandy said. "Could you teach it to me?"

"The angel came," Maddy said. "She said a forever friend would help us all, and she taught us the song. Are you the forever friend sent by the angel?"

"I don't know," Brandy said. "I'm a forever friend. I promised, cross my heart. But I don't know what kind of help you need."

"My Ma's kinda sick," Brad said. "She coughs a lot nowadays. And the men what get friendly with her and give her money don't come around much anymore. Could you cure her?"

97

"Texas men and *vaqueros* ain't here in winter," Juanita said. "So Mama don't get many friends, the kind what pays her a dollar or sometimes two just for being with her for a little while. We gotta get out when men comes."

"Brandy forever friend?"

"Yes, Ted?"

"I'm gonna be six right after Christmas. Can I go to school when I'm six?"

"Bastards like us cain't go to school," Brad said. "You know that. I'm more than eight and Nita's gonna be eight in the summer. You don't see us going to no school, do ya?"

"I know we're bastards," Ted said. "But sure would be good if we could learn how to read some. I'd like that."

"Me, too," Juanita said. "I'm a girl and ain't good for nothing but cleaning, cooking, and poking, but I'd sure like to read something."

"Forever friend," Maddy said. "Could I have a hug?"

Brandy held out her arms. "As many as you want, forever friend. Come here."

When she wrapped little Maddy in her arms Brandy realized how scrawny the little girl was. Now, when she looked at Maddy's face, she would see that only a thin covering of fair skin lay over her bones.

"Come on," she said to the others. "Your forever friend wants to give you all a good hug." She hugged Ted, then Juanita, and, last of all, Brad, though he wasn't sure he wanted a hug. Each hug brought home to her how emaciated the four children were.

With her arms around the children, Brandy said, "Look, the sun's almost out of sight. Your folks will be worried."

"Nah," Brad said. "Night's when the men come. Not good for kids to be in the crib."

"Gets cold after sundown. It's getting cold now," said Brandy. "What are you going to do?"

"Sometimes Mr. Pepper lets us in the back room of Asa's. Sometimes we can get in the loft at Tolliver's livery, but we have to sneak in. It all depends."

"You have to sneak in?" Brandy repeated. "Does Mister Tolliver not let you in? Have you asked him?"

"Ain't no point askin'," Brad said, "it always just gets one more *no*."

Brandy hugged them again. "Try to keep warm." She struggled to keep the tears from her voice. "I'll try to come here again tomorrow."

"Would you?" Maddy said. "Would you? Forever friend, would you?"

"I must go," Brandy said. "How do I say goodbye to the Angel Tree?"

"We have to sing the Angel Tree song again, Brandy, before we go." The children joined hands with Brandy in the middle between Juanita and Ted and sang the song. Then each walked past the tree and dragged a hand lightly across the evergreen leaves. "Until tomorrow," they each said. "Until tomorrow."

Brandy brushed her hand against the Angel Tree last. It seemed like a burst of warmth came from the boughs. "Until tomorrow," she said.

The children took off at a run, little Maddy struggling to keep up. Brandy also took their path through the willow barrier and came out facing the shacks and long houses known as Cribtown. She counted the structures. Thirteen. Dusk deepened, but only three of the thirteen had lights in them. She knew Asa Pepper and Harry Turner had about a dozen working girls in Asa's saloon. She counted the doors on both long houses. Four each. So there were cribs enough for nearly twenty doves. No wonder Miss Abby was upset. Unfair competition, she said. Working as a dove could be dangerous. As Brad said, sometimes customers beat the doves. Sometimes customers didn't pay and the doves had to pay Turner out of their hoard. Brandy knew about that.

The biggest one-room shack stood farthest away from Asa's saloon. And it looked like no one lived there, or even used the place. It sat on the ground with squared logs as its foundation. The door had a cracked leather latchstring, and the single window had three of its four panes cracked or completely broken.

Brandy sidled up to the little shack and knocked timidly on the door.

"Ain't no one what lives there," a raspy female voice said.

Brandy snatched her hand away from the door as if it were red hot. "I wonder whose it is?" she said in a small voice.

"You wanna use it? Just tell Asa Pepper or Harry Turner. It's not like they owns the cribs or nothing, it's just that they keep their finger on every dove what comes down here, soiled or not." The woman walked over to where she could see Brandy well when she raised the little lantern she carried.

Brandy looked down, shading her face with the brim of her bonnet.

"Got smacked, didjer? Your man a smacker?"

"He'll never do it to me again," Brandy said. "Never."

"Some men like to get rough. They pays their money, they thinks they can do any old thing they want." The woman smiled, showing two teeth missing in front. "You gonna move into this crib?"

Brandy wandered away without answering. Her head was spinning.

The next day, after telling Miss Abby, she walked uptown –to the Wolf Creek school. She knocked on the door, and a man answered. She recognized him as the schoolmaster, Marcus Sublette.

"Can I help you, miss?" he said. "I'm sort of in the middle of teaching a class in there."

"You're Mister Sublette," she said.

"I am. I don't think I've had the pleasure."

"I'm Brandy. Yesterday I heard something awful. I heard that the little kids from down below Useless Grant, the ones whose mamas work in the cribs, aren't allowed in your school with –with *decent* kids."

His face reddened. "I've never turned a child away, miss. But the mayor, and the town council –they've made clear that those children are not acceptable company."

Brandy looked him in the eye, and he was clearly embarrassed. "Who's in charge, you or them?"

"I'm the schoolmaster. But they bought the building, and they pay my salary. Besides, some of the other kids –

and their parents, one or two in particular –would make life mighty rough for those poor children even if they tried to come, probably more than I could protect them from."

"Sounds like you don't have much say," Brandy said, her voice cold as ice. "Sounds like you ain't all that different from me, or those kids' mamas. I won't keep you anymore, good day."

She spun on her heel and marched away, leaving the headmaster with red cheeks and downcast eyes.

Brandy walked back to Dogleg City. Things seemed lively, but not yet going full blast. Harvey Turner walked by and Brandy trotted over to stop him with a hand on his arm.

"Well, well, well. If it's not Miss Brandy from the Abby's School for Wayward Women. You wanna come work for me? Might just make more money over here."

"I need to speak to Asa," she said. "Could you call him for me? Please."

Turner gave her a lecherous look, up and down and back up again. "I reckon I could do that. Might lead to something interesting."

Moments later, scrawny Asa Pepper pushed through the door. "You wanting me, Miss Brandy?" His voice was civil, but his face was hard. "Can't think of anything I could do for you. You ain't a crib-type woman."

"Asa. Do you know whose shack that is on the far end of Cribtown? Right now, nobody lives in it."

"That cabin may be the oldest building in all of Wolf Creek, gal. B'longed to the man they called Wolf Killer. Him and Casto Haston was in these parts purt near afore anyone else, 'cept maybe Kiowas."

"Must I ask Casto if I want to use it?"

"You? A crib woman?"

Brandy shook her head. "No. I may be a dove, but not that kind. Hope never to be. But they're people, just like you and me. And they got kids just like other mamas. I want to try to build those children a little school in that cabin."

Asa Pepper's big eyes got even bigger, and a smile tugged at the corners of his normally taciturn mouth. "A school. For Cribtown kids."

Brandy nodded. "And maybe it could be a warm place for them to wait for their mothers to finish working, too."

Pepper let out a bark of a laugh. "I'll be hogwashed. And who's gonna teach at this here school?"

"I don't have everything figured out yet, Asa. But I know it needs to be done. Would you help?"

"You're asking me? A darky? You want *me* to help you?"

"I'm asking because you know what it's like, you know, being on the wrong side of the street."

"What do you want me to do?"

Brandy dug into her pocket and brought out ten half-dimes, two four-bit pieces, a half dollar, and a cartwheel. She held the money out to Asa. "The kids say sometimes you let them stay in the back of your place when it's cold. Could you make sure they get something to eat, too? They're awful skinny."

"You'd buy our kids food? A mulatto, a Meskin, and two poor white trash kids?"

"I know it's not much, Asa. Tell me when it runs out. I'll give you some more. Could you feed them?"

Asa Pepper showed that hint of a smile again. He clutched the coins in his big hand and nodded. "I can do that, Miss Brandy. Don't you worry."

"Thank you, Asa." Brandy turned away, determined to go to the Lucky Break. Then she turned back. "Merry Christmas, Asa. May the angel bless you." Once again she set her course for the Lucky Break.

Billy Below's horse was not tied out front, so Brandy marched east on Useless Grant Street toward the Wolf's Den. Peering in through the window, Brandy could not see Wes Quaid anywhere inside, but fortune follows angels, and she saw him walking down Fifth Street with his usual swagger. Feeling very unladylike, she trotted up the street to meet him. "Wes, oh, Wes."

Quaid came up short. "What in hell . . .? What are you doing around here, Brandy?" Then he noticed her bruised cheek and blackened eye. "Who smacked you, girl. Tell me, and he'll pay. I swear to God, he'll pay."

"Wes. Be a dear and tell Billy Below that I really need to talk to him, could you? You're the only one I can depend on."

"Billy?" Quaid sounded dejected for a second, but only a second. "Sure, I'll tell Billy. And I'll tell you this. Anything you tell Billy, you can tell me. Me and him, we're on the same track, going the same way. Purt near."

Brandy nodded. "All right. When you find Billy, please come to Miss Abby's. I can't work until my bruises don't show, so there will be no charge. No fooling around, either. This is serious and important. Do you understand?"

"I do, Brandy, I surely do. I'll talk to Billy and we'll be over, I promise."

Brandy very nearly made a cross over her heart. "Thank you so much, Wes. I must be off. Miss Abby will be anxious." She turned and strode to Useless Street, turned left, and almost ran back to Miss Abby's house.

As Brandy opened the rear door, Miss Abby shouted, "Mary Wakefield!"

She must be really angry. She never called the girls by their given names. "I'm back, Miss Abby," Brandy called.

"You get in here, right this minute."

Brandy unwound the muffler and took off her bonnet. With some trepidation, she rapped on Miss Abby's door.

"Get in here, girl."

"Yes, Miss Abby." Brandy went hesitantly into Miss Abby's room, the one she called her "office." "I'm here, Miss Abby. I'm sorry to be so late. I just lost track of time. I'm sorry."

"If you have men to meet, you meet them here."

"Yes'm."

"Take your bonnet off. Let me look at your face."

Miss Abby took Brandy by the chin and turned her head this way and that. "Eye still pretty bruised. Cheek's getting better, though. Hmmm. I'd say another week would do it. Then you can get back to work. Several of your admirers have been asking after you."

"Thank you, Miss Abby." Brandy took a deep breath. *Now or never.* "Um, Miss Abby? I was wondering. You keep all my money in trust, don't you? I was wondering. Could I have some of it now? It being almost Christmas, and all."

Miss Abby's head came up like a buck deer smelling trouble. "Don't you think I'll be fair with you?"

"It's not that, Miss Abby. It's just, well . . ." Brandy told Miss Abby all about the condition of Cribtown, and how things were not good for the crib girls, and how the four kids were skinny and cold and wanted to go to school, and that she had figured a way to fix up the Wolf Killer's old cabin into a schoolroom for Cribtown kids, but she didn't say a thing about the Angel Tree. She'd promised not to.

Miss Abby stood for a long moment with her hand rubbing her small jaw. "I'm a Christian woman," she said, "at least I was brought up that way. I can see what you want to do is right. How much will you need?"

"Twenty-five dollars, maybe?"

"That's a lot of whitewash."

"It's Christmas soon, Miss Abby. I never had much Christmas, and maybe that's why I'm here, no offense meant, and I'd like for these Cribtown kids to have one Christmas they won't forget. And if I'm still here next year, another one."

Miss Abby thought some more. "Let's start with ten dollars, Brandy, and use more later if we need to. Keep track of what you use it for, can you do that?"

"Yes, ma'am. Probably. I ain't gone to school but for three years myself."

"You'll do fine. Now, go have your supper. Gentlemen are starting to arrive, and I'd prefer you in your room before we have any men in the waiting room."

"Yes, ma'am. Thank you, ma'am." Brandy rushed to the kitchen, retrieved some sourdough bread, a pat of butter, a pot of crab apple jelly, and a glass of cider. Holding her supper carefully, she ascended to her room.

What a wonderful Christmas it will be around the Angel Tree.

Miss Abby's place did not stir early in the morning. Actually, noon would be a good time to consider visiting if wishing to be "early." Wes Quaid and Billy Below pounded on the front door when the grandfather clock in the foyer had just clanged out the ten o'clock hour. Howie Perkins opened the door enough so the men could see one eye. "Too early for doves to be flyin', gentlemen. Please come back in the afternoon."

"Howie! Dear Howie," Brandy called from the top of the stairway. "Who is it, please?"

"Mr. Quaid and little Billy Below, Miss Brandy."

"Show them to my room, please," Brandy said.

Howie Perkins stood speechless for a moment, then opened the door. "This way, gentlemen," he said.

Quaid didn't wear spurs in town, but Billy's clanked all the way up the stairs and jingled as he walked the few steps to Brandy's room. "Hi, Brandy," he said. He dug a dollar from his pocket. "This is for the sheet you used awhile back when you bandaged my butt."

"Why, thank you, Billy. I didn't think you'd remember." She took the dollar and put it with a pile of coins on her dresser.

"Wes. Billy. Sit on the bed, please. Howie, stand by the door and don't let anyone in. Could you do that?"

Howie pulled out his oak truncheon and smacked it into his palm with a resounding whack. "No one in, Miss Brandy. I'll see to it." He stood spraddle-legged in front of the door, his arms folded, the oak truncheon clutched in his right fist, and a look of determination on his face.

Quaid untied the leg thong of his gun first, then he and Billy Below sat on Brandy's bed.

"What's up, Brandy? Wes said you wanted me, well, me and him, quick as possible. Mr. Breedlove give me the morning off, but I gotta get back to the T Bar B before late afternoon. We're setting up windbreaks for when the snow flies."

"Thanks for coming in, Billy. I know you're busy.

Billy sat forward on the bed, his full attention on Brandy. Quaid sat near the foot, and his eyes drifted restlessly toward the windows as if checking to see nothing dangerous was coming from outside.

Brandy waved at the money on the dresser. "I need things bought, but I don't want a lot of people to know about it. I borrowed ten dollars from Miss Abby, and I added my own savings, like the extra dollar you always give me, Billy. So here's what I need." She told them of the shack and that she needed whitewash for inside and out. And that if there was enough money, to get Joe Nash to put in a wood floor and make a blackboard. "But keep back some of the money to get the kids—you know them, Brad and Juanita and Ted and Maddy—they need some clothes, pants and jackets and such. Asa said he would help, so talk to him, too."

"Damn," Quaid said. "You can fix up a shack into a school room, but who's gonna teach them kids? I mean, I had no ma. I got pushed around to any place that wanted free work for a little food. I first killed a man when I was just past eleven years old. I know lots about guns, but godawful little about the Three Rs."

Billy said nothing for a moment, then, "We can do 'er, Wes. Let's get going."

"I'll be at the new school in the morning, ready to whitewash," Brandy said. "I don't have to work again until Christmas. By then, my black eye will be healed."

"I'll ask you again, Brandy girl," Wes Quaid said. "Who done that?"

"It were Cecil Cranz," Howie Perkins called from the door.

"He's a dead man," Quaid said. He jammed on his hat. "Come on, Mr. Below. We got things to do and people to see."

"Wes. Make me a promise, please."

"What promise, Brandy?"

"Don't kill Cecil Cranz. *Do. Not. Kill. Him.* Promise?"

"If you say," Quaid said, and left.

Billy put his Stetson on firmly, leaned over to give Brandy a quick kiss on the cheek, "Rest easy, Brandy girl, we'll get 'er done," he said, then followed Quaid, who was already halfway down the stairs.

As soon as Quaid and Billy had gone, Howie said, "Can I come to Christmas, too?"

"Of course, Howie. I'll send you a special invitation."

"I can't read."

"That's no problem. I'll hand it to you personally."

"I'll thank you for that, Miss Brandy." Howie's smile was as big as those on the children at the Angel Tree.

Brandy worked, oh how she worked, while the blackish bruises around her eye turned yellow and disappeared. After cleaning the Wolf Killer cabin inside and out, she started whitewashing. And once that was done, Joe Nash showed up to put in a wood floor. "Nothing fancy," he said. "Just some leftover cottonwood." But when he finished, it was a real workmanlike wood floor. He fixed the broken window, too. "I'll bring you a blackboard later, and whip up some slates. Half-dozen enough?" He never said a word about money.

As she was hanging curtains after the whitewash had dried, she heard footsteps coming toward the door. A young man with sandy hair cut very short and laughing gray eyes stuck his head in. "Top o' the morning to you, lass. A very small bird spoke in me ear this morning and said an angel was building a school in Cribtown, it did. And might you be the angel?"

"I'm no angel, and folks around here call me Brandy. And yes, I hope to turn this cabin into a school for Cribtown children. Do you want to help, or have you come to make fun of me?"

"Make fun? Of an angel? Never on your life, lass. Me name's Sean Flannery, and I'm from Dublin on the Emerald Isle. Most people call me Father Flannery—I prefer Father Sean, but I think they need to get a little more comfortable with me, first. I hope I can be Father Sean to you.. Now. How would you put me to work?"

"You're Catholic, then?"

"I am. I'm to build a mission here in Wolf Creek, but as yet have no more than a room at the boarding house. So when I heard of the angel, I hurried over to help." The laughter never left Father Sean's eyes for a moment, and Brandy felt absolutely safe with him there.

"But why in the world would you think me an angel? Uptown they call us 'soiled doves,' and cross to the other side of the street when they see us coming. Not an angel at all. You can mix whitewash and apply it to the outside of the cabin, please."

"I'll need water, Miss Brandy. Where should I go to find it?"

"Wolf Creek. Where else?"

Father Sean wandered away, whistling, with two buckets in his hands. A few minutes later, he stuck his head in and said, "Whitewash? Brushes?"

"In the lean-to out back."

"By the way, I heard some children singing while I was at the creek. Couldna make out the words, but a beautiful tune it was."

Brandy smiled. "The children of Cribtown," she said. "The angels you were looking for."

"Inasmuch as ye have done it unto one of the least of these my brethren," Father Sean said, "ye have done it unto me."

"What's that?"

"Oh, just a little part of the Bible that I happen to like a good deal." He carried the buckets of water around back, mixed the whitewash, and was soon whistling and singing as he whitewashed the weathered gray sides of the cabin.

"We'll need a sign on the cabin to let people know it's a school, won't we?" Father Sean said, but so many things demanded Brandy's attention that she gave it no further thought.

Two days before Christmas, Brandy met with her forever friends at the Angel Tree. They sang the Angel

Tree song and say on the brown grass. Brandy held Maddy on her lap. "Our Angel Tree is so special," Brandy said. "I was thinking. Wouldn't it be nice to invite Mr. Pepper and Mr. Hunter, your mothers and the other women in Cribtown, and whoever else you want to come to the Angel Tree on Christmas Morning? You could sing the Angel Tree song and some Christmas songs, and maybe I could make a Christmas cake at Miss Abby's, and bring that. Does that sound fun?"

The children clapped. "Real Christmas cake," Maddy said. "That makes me so happy. Forever friends are wondrous."

"I have one more idea," Brandy said. "What would you like best in the world to make for your mother? Something that you could make all by yourself."

"A piece of your cake would be good," Maddy said.

Brandy smiled. "Thank you, dear little Maddy. But not something *I* made, something *you* made. Wouldn't that be great? Think about it, and we'll talk when we meet tomorrow."

Everyone agreed, and joined hands around the decorated boxwood, singing the Angel Tree song.

It snowed on Christmas Eve. Not a blowing blistering blizzard of a snow storm, but a soft soundless sky full of floating flake clusters, big as the feathers that flew about during pillow fights.

On Christmas Morning, the land lay almost spotless in white. As Brandy left Miss Abby's with her hand basket, Howie Perkins was not in his customary place in the drawing room. Brandy thought nothing of it. In her basket, Brandy had the Christmas pound cake she'd baked under the watchful eye of Ho Gah Ling, the Chinese cook. It even had icing made from powdered sugar, whipped egg whites, and water. It had hardened up nicely, and Brandy had a sharp butcher knife in the bottom of the basket she'd use to cut the cake for the children. What a surprise! They knew nothing of Brandy's plan.

She put on coat and woolen muffler, rubber boots and bonnet. As she left Miss Abby's, she hummed the Angel Tree song. Hers were the first tracks in the new-fallen snow. At least until she crossed Useless Street and went down the bank toward Wolf Creek. There she noticed tiny prints of birds, the dot-dash tracks of rabbits that had moved back and forth among the willow trees.

The children were already at the Angel Tree when Brandy got there. They squatted in a semicircle on the uphill side of the tree, their small red hands steepled and their heads bowed. Brandy stopped at the edge of the willows and waited until they raised their heads.

"Hi, forever friends," she said, her voice bubbling. "Merry Christmas."

They turned, and Brandy noticed tears in their eyes. Not streaks of tears, just tears that threatened to tumble over their lower lids. "Oh? Crying? On Christmas morning?"

The children said nothing.

Brandy folded her arms around the basket. "Can't you tell me? I'm your forever friend, right?"

Maddy jumped up, ran to Brandy, and buried her face in Brandy's skirt, sobbing and clutching the material in her little fists.

113

Brandy squatted, put the basket on the snow-covered ground, and hugged Maddy. "What's wrong, dear Maddy? What's wrong? Now, now, stop crying and tell me."

Maddy hiccupped and wiped her eyes on the back of her hands. "Forever friend. She didn't do it. She didn't do anything."

Brandy reached inside the basket and pulled out an old blanket. "Brad, Juanita. Here. Spread this out so we can sit on it. Brush away the snow first, please."

The older children did as Brandy asked and soon all five forever friends sat on the blanket, their arms around their knees, looking at the Angel Tree. The little evergreen glistened in the morning light. White snow clung to its green leaves, and decorations of red, yellow, and orange strings and bits of cloth seemed to make the little tree smile.

"So beautiful, the Angel Tree," Brandy whispered.

Juanita started singing the Angel Tree song, and everyone else joined in. When they finished, Brandy said, "Who is 'she' and what didn't she do?"

"We asked the angel for gifts," Brad said. "Not stuff for us. Stuff for our moms and other people. Them without coats or shoes or warm scarves."

"Lookee," Maddy pointed at the Angel Tree. "They's nothing there. Nothing."

Brandy couldn't hold back the tears. "Oh dear. Oh dear. We have to believe, though. Didn't an angel teach you the Angel Tree song?"

The children nodded.

"Then let's sing the Angel Tree song again, all together. Just trust in the angel, and then we'll have a nice piece of Christmas cake."

"Cake?"

Brandy smiled. "Yes. Cake."

Again, Juanita started the song, and they all joined in. When they finished, four now-eager faces looked up at Brandy.

"I baked it last night," Brandy said. She reached into the basket and brought out something wrapped in a clean cotton flour sack. Then she got the butcher knife. "Christmas is a special day. Everyone's supposed to be happy on Christmas. It celebrates the birth of baby Jesus. I don't have candles, because it's been one thousand eight hundred and seventy-one years since He was born, and there's not that many candles in all of Wolf Creek. Shall we celebrate? Eat some cake for baby Jesus?"

"Yaaay!"

Brandy cut the cake—simple pound cake with fluffy white icing—and gave each child a slice, which they held carefully with both hands. They looked expectantly at Brandy. She cut a slice for herself and picked it up. "Who would like to thank God for cake on Christmas?" she asked. "He is our Father in Heaven."

No one spoke. Then Maddy said in a very small voice, "I will."

"Thank you, Maddy. Everybody, bow your heads. Maddy's going to thank Heavenly Father for the Christmas cake."

Four heads bowed. "Father way up there," Maddy said. "Thank you. Forever friend made the cake, but thank you anyway." She opened one eye and looked up at Brandy, who mouthed *amen.*

Maddy bowed her head again and said, "Amen. Oh. And happy birthday, Jesus."

"Can we eat the cake now?" Brad asked.

"Of course," Brandy said.

Four mouths opened, and large portions of pound cake with icing disappeared into them. Four youngsters smiled as the sweetness and smooth texture of Christmas pound cake gave them a brand new experience. "I've never tasted anything so heavenly," Juanita said, and took another bite.

"Listen," Ted said. "Someone's singing."

Indeed the sound of Christmas carols came from the direction of Cribtown. Chewing stopped.

O little town of Bethlehem, how still we see thee lie . . .

"They're singing that new Christmas song," Brandy said.

The children stood, straining to see who was coming, but the willows hid the singers.

The music changed. *Deck the halls with boughs of holly . . .*

Maddy jumped up and down. "The holly song. The holly song." She laughed, and it sounded like the tinkling of bells.

Father Sean pushed through the willows. "Merry Christmas, dear friends," he said. "May we come to see your Angel Tree? We have songs to sing and presents to give, and love to share with all. May we come in?"

"Yaaay."

Behind Father Sean came the mothers of Brandy's forever friends. The four women wore high-necked dresses with bloused sleeves. Two wore bonnets, and two had wool scarves. The rest of the Cribtown doves followed, all in normal clothing. Asa Pepper and Harry Turner pushed through the willows, then some other men who patronized Asa's Saloon—Alvin Cook, Wilfred Barnes, Ajax Brown, and more.

"All of ye. Spread out around the clearing now." Father Sean herded everyone into a group that faced the children across the Angel Tree. "Are ye ready now?" Father Sean raised his arms like an orchestra director, and when he signaled, everyone began to sing. *We three kings of Orient are. Bearing gifts we traverse afar . . .*

Into the clearing came Billy Below, and Wesley Quaid, and Jimmy Spotted Owl, and Howie Perkins, followed by Dave Benteen the gunsmith, Spike Sweeney and Emory Charleston from the blacksmith shop, Joe Nash the carpenter, Toy Sullivan from the freight office, Li Wong and Jing Jing from the laundry, and the schoolteachers Marcus Sublette and Cora Sloane.

"Our blacksmiths have been hunting," Father Sean said, "and think they've found something important you ought to see."

"Wait," Brandy said. She dug four small packages from her baskets. "I wrapped your presents for your mothers. Do you want to give them now?"

The four Cribtown children stood before their mothers, and it was easy to tell which child belonged to whom. Brad's mother was quadroon, and Juanita's had the dark beauty of Mexico. Ted and Maddy's mothers were blond and fair, though working in Cribtown left them pale and wrinkled beyond their years.

"I made it," Brad said. "It's a hot pot holder."

"My gift to you, my mother, is a cross, like the one where Jesus died. I made it myself." Juanita's mother pulled her daughter into her arms and wept into her hair.

"Brandy helped," Ted said. "It's for the coffee pot. Something to put it on."

"I love you, Mommy," Maddy said. "My forever friend helped me make a pin cushion heart for you."

"What were you saying about Spike and Emory, Father Sean?" Brandy said.

"Aye, lassie. They've found a very important gift, they say. But it cannot be carried all the way to the Angel Tree. We must go to it. Gentlemen?" Father Sean beckoned to the big ex-slave and the lithe white man in the Confederate cap. "Come," he said. "Lead the children to the place you found."

"I think you gonna like it," Em said, and Spike nodded with a smile

"What is it?" she asked.

"Can we go with you?" Maddy said.

"Of course. Let's follow and to see what they have found." Brandy took Maddy and Ted by the hand and led them after Spike and Em. Maddy held out her other hand for Juanita, and Brad followed close behind. Through the willows the blacksmiths went, with Brandy and the children close behind, followed by Father Sean, who had a knowing smile on his face, the children's mothers, and the citizens of Wolf Creek who had gathered at the Angel Tree that Christmas Morning of 1871.

The morning sun seemed to concentrate on the Wolf Killer's cabin. Its sides were brilliant white. Its shingles showed signs of repair. New windowpanes graced the newly painted window frame. Emory Charleston marched right up to the cabin. At the door, he stopped, and turned to face those who followed him.

"That's the cabin Brandy's been whitewashing," Brad said. "What's that got to do with Christmas?"

"A lot more than you might think," Spike said.

When everyone had gathered around, Emory held his hands up for silence. "You all might think this is Wolf Killer's cabin, the oldest one in all of Wolf Creek, and you'd be right. But Miss Brandy fixed it up, with help from a bunch of people. I'd tell you who they all are, but that's not what Christmas is all about."

He cleared his throat and spat off to the side. "'Scuse," he said. "Now. Miss Brandy fixed up old Wolf Killer's cabin for a reason. And she cleared it with ever'body." Emory reached for a board that leaned against the whitewashed cabin. He turned it over and held it up so everyone could see.

It was a sturdy thing, with words carefully and boldly carved into it. Brandy immediately recognized the handicraft of Joe Nash, the quiet carpenter. She cast a glance at him and he looked away, embarrassed.

"What does it say?" Maddy said. "Something's written on it." She jerked at Brandy's hand. "What's it say, forever friend. Huh? What's writ on it?"

"It says . . . it says . . ." Brandy's voice caught and she couldn't go on.

Father Sean went over to Emory Charleston. He grasped one end of the board and they lifted it high above their heads so everyone could see. "This is the sign that will go over the door of this cabin. This is the sign that will open the way to the future for many a youngster on the south side of Ulysses S. Grant Street. It reads: Angel Tree School."

"Angel Tree School?" Maddy said.

"That's right."

"What kind of school?" Juanita asked.

"A school for you, and for Brad, and for Ted, and when Maddy gets to be six years old, she can go to school here, too. Come in. See what there is for you." Father Sean led the way into the cabin while Emory hung the sign over the door.

Inside they found desks, slates, a blackboard . . . everything a school needed but one thing. There was no teacher.

"Well? What do you think?" Father Sean asked.

"Hmm. It really would be good to learn how to read and write, and work sums," Brad said. "But where's the teacher?"

Brandy stood in the doorway, watching the children.

"Forever friend? Could you be the teacher?" Maddy said.

"Dear Maddy. I could teach you the alphabet, maybe, but that's about all."

Brandy looked hesitantly toward Marcus Sublette and Cora Sloane, both of whom were smiling. She asked them a silent question with her eyes, but Marcus smiled even broader and shook his head.

"Oh, but the Angel Tree School has a teacher," Marcus said. "A fully qualified teacher. But it's not either of us."

"Then who?" Brandy said.

Father Flannery stepped forward. "I'm willing to shoulder the burden part of the time, my child, but I am counting on you to help me. And Mister Sublette has agreed to help us get set up, give us some direction on how to go about this venture."

"It's my pleasure," Marcus said. "I've been thinking a lot since our earlier conversation, Brandy. It doesn't really matter what the 'town fathers' want, it just matters what's right. I'm not just going to help you all get set up, I've been talking with someone over in Matthias, to see about getting them a teacher and a school as well."

The priest grinned. "Some of those 'town fathers' view you and me in the same light, Brandy, but it's little we care."

Father Sean's merry face turned serious. "I'm from Ireland. A bonny country that's under the thumb of the British. They don't think of the worth of a man there. Or a woman. Or of much anything else, it seems sometimes. But here, way back in 1776, this country declared independence from Britain. And in the declaration that Tom Jefferson wrote, it says: We hold these truths to be self-evident, that all men are created equal . . ."

Father Sean stepped over to stand in front of Brandy. He took her hands in his. "Thank you, dear Brandy, for showing me that all the people who get frowned at when they go north of Useless Street are equal to anyone else, in God's eyes." He held Brandy's hand high. His voice carried to the farthest person. "This Christmas, Mary Wakefield, the woman we affectionately know as Brandy, gave four small children a precious gift. The opportunity for education. We named this cabin Angel Tree School,

121

and Brandy is the one who made it happen." He turned to Brandy. "Thank you, Mary," he said. "You are an angel."

Brandy wept.

THE END

THE SPIRIT OF HOGMANAY

Clay More

"It's me again, Doctor Munro, sir," said young Billy Tanner as Logan opened his surgery door in answer to the knock. A flurry of snow blew in past Billy, who stood holding a wooden crate.

"Come in, Billy. You've been busy this Christmas, what with finding bodies in the snow and now delivering crates."

Logan closed the door after the teenager and then led the way through to his consulting room.

"Put the crate on that table in the corner, would you. I'll just get a hammer to open it."

Billy did as he was asked and stood rubbing his bare hands together to try and warm them up. He was a bright-eyed youngster of fifteen with a shock of red hair and a face full of freckles. His face naturally fell into a smile to reveal healthy white teeth. He was wiry in build, which Logan attributed to both nature and a diet that was probably lacking in sustenance half the time. That went with the bedraggled, hand-me down clothes that were a tad too big for him as evidenced by the turn-ups of pant bottoms and jacket sleeves.

Logan came back with a hammer and used the claw to grasp one of the nails that held its lid to the crate.

As he did so, Billy pointed at the label. "Folks just don't respect what they see with their own eyes, do they, Doctor Munro? I mean, that notice there clearly says

123

HANDLE WITH CARE, yet it's been scuffed, scratched and dented. You can see the wood is a bit broken on the side right there where it has your name and address on it."

He shook his head and then proceeded to emphasize both the name and address. "Doctor Logan Munro, Wolf Creek, Kansas, United States of America. Now any fool could work out it is probably a crate full of medicines that's come from overseas, yet there they went throwing and tossing it around the place. I only hope that whatever's inside isn't all broke."

Logan had a soft spot for the youngster, who had only been a resident of Wolf Creek for about six months, when he had been sent by relatives back East, to stay with his grandfather. From what Logan knew, his parents had died of typhus and Billy had been taken in by an aunt until he proved one mouth too many to feed.

Although he hadn't had all that many contacts with him, on the occasions that he had, he had been impressed by his powers of observation and his obvious intelligence.

Back in the early fall Marcus Sublette, the school head teacher, had asked Logan to go in and hold a biology class for the older kids. Logan had done so, taking half-a-dozen bull's eyes, which he had obtained from Frank Kloepfer, the butcher. Logan had supplied some scissors and scalpels and shown them how to dissect the eyeball, to show them how it was all made up. He had shown them the aqueous humor at the front of the eye, the lens that focused light onto the retina at the back of the eye and the yellow jelly of the vitreous humor.

Most of the kids had either shied away in disgust or made a hash of the dissection. Except for Billy. He had shown real interest in learning all about the eye and the way that it was operated by the optic muscles. Yet the thing that impressed Logan most was Billy's dexterity. He had steady and adept hands. The sort of hands that he felt were made by God to do something skillful. He was a natural dissector.

He just hoped that he would have the opportunity to make something of himself in life. Yet, as he looked now at Billy's baggy and woefully inadequate clothing for the Kansas winter, he had doubts that would ever be the case. Not without a lot of luck.

Logan pulled out the last of the nails and then raised the lid. Inside was a heavy padding of straw, which he removed to reveal a dozen large bottles of liquid.

"A colleague of mine in Glasgow, that's a city in Scotland, sent this consignment out," he explained, lifting bottles one at a time to check them for breakages. "Most of these contain a five per cent solution of a wonderful thing called carbolic acid. It is the surgeon's best friend, Billy."

He pulled two more out, which were clearly quite different from the others. Satisfied that they were undamaged, he held one up to the light to examine the square label. "And these four," he said, pointing with the one in his hand to three others in the crate, "have come all the way from Ballindalloch in the Highlands of Scotland."

He grinned. "And you could say that this is the finest medicine in the world. Back home we call it *'uisgebeatha,'* which means *'water of life.'* This is single malt whisky called *The Glenlivet,* and it is in my opinion the very best that there is. They have been distilling it for a quarter

125

century before I was born. I was hoping it would arrive before Hogmanay."

He replaced the bottle and pulled out one of the clear bottles of carbolic acid. Then he reached into his pocket and fished out a coin. "This is for your trouble, Billy." He flicked it toward Billy, who caught it and pocketed it with the dexterity of a conjurer.

"Thanks, Doctor Munro. I'll put it to good use."

"I'm sure you will, son." He pointed at Billy's feet. "Might I suggest socks. You'll get chilblains in this weather. Now, I am afraid that I must go. Mrs. Pomeroy is waiting for me with my patient."

"Will Mr. Koepfler be okay?" Billy asked.

"I am going to have to operate on him, but he is lucky that you found him lying in the snow down by the Creek. If he had been out there much longer he could well have been dead by now. His poor wife, Anna, had Marshall Sam Gardner and his deputies searching all over for him when he didn't come home overnight and all the next day."

***

Doctor Logan Munro had only given Frank Kloepfer enough chloroform to produce light anesthesia. He was worried that the patient may not have coped with too much, for he was not in the best of shape and he had known cases when men of his great bulk had simply stopped breathing and died.

"Are you sure that you are okay, Martha?" he asked the handsome woman who was standing beside him with swabs at the ready, as he grasped the patient's foot and positioned his scalpel ready to make an incision. "There will be some blood and when I actually get to the bone there will be some disagreeable noise."

Martha Pomeroy's face seemed paler than usual and she had tears in her eyes, yet she still managed to give him a wan smile. "It is this carbolic acid that you have washed his foot in and soaked your instruments with. It is making my eyes water and it makes the back of my throat rasp. Apart from that I am fine. I have seen plenty of blood before, Doctor Munro. I've watched you deliver enough of the ladies of Wolf Creek to be hardened to it."

Logan hefted the scalpel in his hand and nodded. He noted the way that she always addressed him by his title when they were involved in anything professionally.

"This carbolic acid solution is changing the whole face of surgery," he explained. "Professor Lister at Glasgow University has been achieving fantastic results with it. I have been following his papers in the *British Medical Journal,* and one of my old colleagues sent me out a consignment."

Without more ado, for he was conscious that he had to work swiftly before the chloroform wore off and before the tourniquet that he had applied restricted blood flow to the foot for too long, he made an elliptical incision around the outer two toes of the left foot. The ends of both toes were black with gangrene and they smelled putrid. As an ooze of blood appeared along the cut margins the smell of blood added to the rancid odor.

Such smells meant nothing to Logan, for he had smelled much worse on the battlefields of three continents.

With a toothed forceps, he lifted the proximal skin edge and began freeing the underlying fascia from the deeper tissues with the back of his scalpel. Having thus exposed the tendons he then divided them and deftly ligated the blood vessels with catgut sutures.

"Swab here, please," he said, pointing to the severed tendons and blood vessels around the exposed bone.

Martha applied the swabs, then moved her hand away once the area was dabbed clean.

"This is the noisy bit," he warned her as he picked up a saw.

"Just do it, Doctor. I'm not listening," she replied, eyeing the next instrument waiting in the row on the table. "It's not the sawing I mind too much, it's the rasping noise you make after it as you file the bone edges."

***

Ten minutes later Frank Kloepfer had woken up and was sitting back against a pile of pillows that Martha had placed on the operating table while Logan had held him up.

Frank Kloepfer, the Wolf Creek butcher, was a big man in his mid-forties who had emigrated from Heidelberg in Germany when he was twenty years old. Like so many Germans from the south of his country, he settled in Milwaukee—where his skills as a butcher enabled him to get work. When the War began, he enlisted in the 9th Wisconsin Volunteer Infantry Regiment under Colonel Frederick C. Salmon, himself a German. Then, when the War was over and he was discharged, he found his way to Wolf Creek, where he took up his former calling as a butcher.

Logan liked the big German butcher, whose luxurious black mustache barely concealed the gap where his two front teeth had been knocked out by an irate customer who had the temerity to imply that he had been sold rancid meat. That had been before the big German had dislocated the man's jaw. It had been Logan's tricky job to reset the jaw.

"*Ach*, Doctor Munro, but that foot hurts like hell!" he exclaimed, pointing at the heavy bandage that Logan had applied to cover the foot. "I dreamed that I had sawn off my foot. I heard the sound of bone being sawn through. As a butcher, I know the sound well."

He saw Martha Pomeroy wince and despite his discomfort, the big butcher's eyes twinkled.

"That is some Christmas present the good doctor has given me, Mrs. Pomeroy.*Ja*? And it smells good, no? Like soap."

Martha smiled non-committally, for she had not enjoyed the sound of the bone ends being smoothed with a file before Logan had drawn the skin flaps over the ends and sewn them closed.

Logan was toweling his hands dry. "I think you had too good a Christmas, Frank. Too much beer and whiskey."

Frank shrugged his shoulders. "This American beer is not like the real beer we make back home in Germany. It is not even as good as the stuff my countrymen make in Milwaukee, so what is a man to do? You need to drink a whiskey with it to get the kick." He shrugged again. "But I admit, I drank too much and fell asleep in the snow. And now I will have to face Anna and try to explain."

Logan shook his head and smiled. The fact was that Frank Kloepfer was always good-humored. He had heard

the hubbub around town when the butcher had
disappeared, but unlike some of the more malicious
tongue-waggers who speculated that he had either holed
up with a woman someplace or high-tailed it out of his
responsibilities, Logan knew that he would never have left
his wife and his two youngsters, Klaus and Renate.

"You are incorrigible, Frank. You slept in the snow for
a whole day. You are lucky to be alive. But as I told you,
those toes had gone gangrenous and had to be amputated,
otherwise it would have spread and I would have to have
taken off your foot. I already told Anna and prepared her."

Frank stroked his mustache contemplatively. "*Ja*! I
must make it all up to her. And I must properly thank that
young man who found me." He shook his head. "I can't
remember what I was doing down at Wolf Creek."

Logan smiled and handed him a small conical shaped
jar. "And now I'll need you to pass me a sample of your
urine."

Frank looked shocked.

"You want me to piss in that? But...what about ...Mrs.
Pomeroy?"

Martha had just finished tidying away all of the blood-
soaked swabs and had wrapped the two amputated toes in
a flannel. "I'm just going now, Mr.Kloepfer, so you can do
what you have to do without any embarrassment." She
turned to Logan and held up the flannel bundle. "What
would you like me to do with this, Doctor Munro?"

"Leave it there, Martha and I'll see to it. It will have to
be incinerated later."

Then as she turned to go he caught her arm. "Martha, I
wonder if I could see you later?" He stared into her dark

eyes and for a moment he said nothing. She had that effect on him, just as he was aware that he had the same effect on her.

Martha Pomeroy was an attractive war widow who lived opposite Wil Marsh's photographic studio at the junction of Lincoln and Fifth Street. She happened to be the best midwife and nurse he had ever worked with, despite the fact that she had no professional training. It was her personal sadness that her husband had been killed at Baxter Springs and she had a stillbirth shortly after.

Logan had also been widowed, having lost Helen, his wife, during the Indian Mutiny when he had served as a surgeon with the British East India Company Army. Thus, both of them had a personal tragedy that they had yet to entirely come to terms with, so they contented themselves with a smile and an understanding that perhaps one day they might mean more to each other.

A nervous smile hovered over her lips. "Of course, Doctor Munro. Is it anything important?"

"It is. I have something I would like to ask you. Perhaps I could call on you tomorrow, or the day after?"

She gave a demure smile then opened the door.

Once she had gone, Frank Kloepfer laughed. "I may just be a drunken old butcher, but I can spot romance in the air, Doctor Munro. Now, if you want my opinion, you should—"

"Just give me the sample, Frank."

There were some medical tasks that Logan Munro did not relish. Tasting urine was one of them, but five minutes later, having done just that he stood with the conical jar containing Frank's urine and rubbed his chin.

"I thought so, Frank. It wasn't just the fact that you fell asleep in the snow, after having drunk goodness knows how much whiskey, that caused you to get frostbitten toes and then rampant gangrene. You've got diabetes mellitus."

"What the hell is that?"

"It's a disease that makes your urine taste sweet. Why it does that no-one knows, except it does. Taste it yourself?"

Frank looked doubtful, but took the jar and raised it to his lips and took a sip. Then he grinned. "Damn! You are right. It is sweet, like honey water."

"Have you been passing a lot of urine lately?"

"I have, now that you ask. All the time. And I get damned thirsty too, and not just for whiskey." He grimaced. "I've had kind of a hankering for water!" He laughed. "How's that, Doctor, Frank's hankering for water?"

"Except it isn't funny, Frank. This disease affects your blood vessels. That's why you got the gangrene."

The enormity of the news began to dawn on Frank. "So what can I do? You can give me some medicine to cure it, can't you, Doc?"

"I'm afraid not," Logan replied. "There is no cure." He reached for Frank's wrist and felt for his pulse. Then he took out his gold Hunter pocket watch and shook it. "Blast, it's stopped working. I'll need to see if I can get it mended. A doctor needs his watch to take pulses."

"Is there nothing I can do, then?"

"There is. I've been reading about the work of a Dr.ApollinaaireBouchardat, a French physician. He says that going on a diet and stopping drinking alcohol can keep it under control. He saw this during the war the French just had with the Prussians. Patients with diabetes improved when food was in short supply."

Frank looked crestfallen. "Godammit, Doc! Couldn't you have picked a better time to tell me this? It's Christmas!"

He frowned and pointed to his foot. "Will I be able to walk on this thing?"

"You will once I give you some laudanum to kill the pain, so that we can get your boot back on. But it's deep with snow outside and I don't want you to get it wet. Go straight home, go to bed and stay there. I'll visit you tomorrow. And no drinking, no sweet things to eat, and only have half as much food as normal. Those are doctor's orders."

Frank pointed at the watch that Logan was still holding. "If I were you I'd go see Linus Zubriggin. He's the best damned watch and clock doctor in town." He shook his head. "Come to think of it, he's the only one. Let's just call that information my little Christmas gift to you."

Then he shook his head sadly. "I cannot believe that you are telling me this. To eat less.Me, a butcher who supplies only the finest meat in Wolf Creek."

***

After lending Frank a walking stick and making sure that he could walk well enough, Logan had shown him through the already crowded waiting room and escorted him out of the door. The boardwalk had been cleared of snow, but a farther light fall had left a slippery patina of white upon it. Piles of snow ran the length of Washington

Street and the road itself had been churned into a slushy, muddy morass by wagons, horses and countless walkers.

"Straight home, Frank," Logan ordered. "And no detours to any of the saloons. You only have two blocks to walk."

"*Ja*, it is straight to bed for me, Doc," the butcher assured him over his shoulder. "See you tomorrow."

Logan slowly along, then returned to his waiting-room. A cursory glance at the pained faces and the way some folk were nursing limbs told him that he had a busy time ahead of him.

He sighed inwardly, but covered it with a reassuring smile at his waiting patients. The days after Christmas were always like this. Either he was dealing with folks suffering from the excesses of the festivity or from some trauma occasioned by the falls in the snow. Sore heads, belly-aches and broken bones, that was what Christmas added to his workload. Or extra surgery such as he had just carried out on Frank Kloepfer. Or an unexpected dying patient to look after, like Fergus the fur trapper who he had accommodated in his hut. Thinking of that patient brought back the line of thought that made him want to see Martha Pomeroy again. Yet it would just have to wait.

"Well folks, I trust you have all had a good Christmas," he said with a smile. "Now who's first?"

***

By the time Logan reached the last patient of the surgery, he was feeling both tired and hungry. Still, his interest was always stimulated when a difficult case presented itself to test his diagnostic skills.

Andre Duquesne was the chef that Richard Wilhite had recently employed at The Imperial Hotel. He was French-born and had worked at a succession of the finest restaurants and hotels in New Orleans before moving to Kansas, seemingly because Richard had offered a sizable financial enticement to secure his services. And since he had arrived, the restaurant at The Imperial Hotel had started to rival that of Isabella's Restaurant. Now, Wolf Creek had both French and Italian cuisine on offer to its citizenry.

But Andre was struggling, as Logan could see before he even examined him. He was a dapper little man with a beeswaxed mustache, twisted and turned up at the ends and with his dark hair brilliantined down glossy and smooth. Logan estimated that he was perhaps fifty years old.

"How long have you been breathless, like this, Andre?"

"*J'ai eu des episodes d'essoufflement pendant environ six semaines,*" Andre replied. "Pardon, Docteur, when I speak with other Europeans I often lapse into French. I meant—"

"I understood, Andre. You have been having bouts of breathlessness for about six weeks. And have they been getting worse?"

"Yes, the more active I am the worse it gets. If I am just cooking, I am all right. And over the last two or three weeks, my ankles have started to swell up. And every now and then my heart starts racing and it feels like I have a hammer in my chest."

135

Logan pointed to the couch and the Frenchman climbed up. Then Logan examined his ankles and found that they were indeed swollen and that when he pressed on the swelling he left an imprint.

"You are retaining fluid, Andre," he said. "We call this pitting edema. Let me listen to your heart."

And uncoiling his stethoscope he listened over the front of his chest. Then he sat him forward, pulled up his shirt and percussed his chest by laying one hand flat on the chest and then tapped on the middle joint of the middle finger with the middle finger of his other. He repositioned his hands several times and percussed all over. Then he listened with his stethoscope again and got him to whisper the words ninety-nine.

Finally, he faced him and reached for his wrist to take his pulse. Automatically, he pulled out his gold Hunter watch to time it. And as before, he shook it and then with a sigh, put it back in his vest pocket.

"I need to get this fixed," he said. "A doctor without a good pulse measuring watch is not a great deal of use." Then, before Andre cold get a question out:

"Tell me, Andre. Did you ever have scarlet fever when you were a youngster?"

The Frenchman nodded. "*Mais oui.* I was ill when I was thirteen."

"Then that settles it. You damaged your heart valves when you were a youngster. You have a narrowed mitral valve and your heart is fibrillating. That means it is not beating as it should and you are starting to get heart failure."

Andre blanched. "That...that sounds bad, *docteur*."

"It means that you will have to take care of yourself, Andre. Don't over-exert yourself. But I can help the symptoms. I am going to give you some pills of digitalis and a potion of Nux vomica, which will act as a tonic on your heart. I will explain the full dosage to you once I make it all up. They will take two or three days to settle the heart down, but they will make you feel a lot better and the swelling in the ankles will disappear. You'll need to stay in bed for a couple of days, because you might feel sick and dizzy as the drugs start to act. That means no work."

Andre slapped his forehead. "*Mon dieu!* Richard Wilhite will not be happy."

"He'd be even less happy if you keeled over and died in his kitchen! I'll be visiting you in your room twice a day, so I'll sort it out with him."

Andre looked relieved. "If you do this, *docteur*, I will think you are a magician." He smiled as he did up his shirt buttons. "And you did not even need your watch to tell this?"

"The signs are quite clear, but I need my watch repaired."

"Then Linus Zubriggin is the man that you must see. He is a Swiss gentleman. He is another European, like us. I haven't seen him around for a while, but—"

"Actually, you are the second person that has mentioned him to me today, Andre."

The French chef swung his legs off the couch and stood up. "Then surely it is meant that you should visit him, *docteur*."

Logan tapped his vest pocket containing the watch.

"I'll do just that, Andre," he said as he went over to his medicine cabinet and took out the bottles and apparatus he needed to prepare the digitalis pills. "Take a seat in the waiting room, Andre. Give me ten minutes and I'll make these pills and the potion up for you."

***

It proved to be a long day with a couple of unexpected emergency visits, so Logan had been unable to visit Linus Zubriggin's shop down at the junction of Fifth and Grant Streets. After a late dinner at Isabella's Restaurant he had gone home, struck a light to his meerschaum pipe, and read a couple of back copies of medical journals that he had been meaning to go through, since they contained articles about a condition that he was preparing a medical paper on.

It was cold, despite the potbellied stove in his sitting room, and he suddenly had a hankering for a Glenlivet malt whisky.

He laid his pipe and the journals aside and went through to his consulting room, where he had left the crate containing his latest consignment.

"Well, I'll be damned!" he exclaimed as he opened the crate and drew back the straw.

There were only two bottles of whisky. Two were missing.

***

The following morning after surgery, Logan called in to see Frank Kloepfer. He found him sitting in his living quarters behind his shop at the corner of Fourth and Washington streets. He was sitting with his heavily bandaged foot up and he was drinking from a mug.

138

Anna Kloepfer had greeted Logan and thanked him profusely for dealing with Frank as she showed him into the room. Then after kissing her husband's head and then paradoxically bestowing a scowl of consternation on him she left the doctor and patient.

Logan picked up the mug and sniffed it. "Just making sure that it is neither sweet, nor alcoholic," he said with a smile. "Beef tea, I am impressed. Now, how does the foot feel?"

"It feels like I lost two toes and I feel a stupid oaf for getting drunk and passing out in the snow. I don't know how I am going to cope with the shop when I open it up tomorrow. I can't afford to lose any more business. I must be about the only shop closed and it is three days after Christmas."

"Yes, most places are open as usual," Logan remarked as he washed his hands in a basin with some of his carbolic acid solution. After toweling them dry he kneeled down and undid the bandage to look at the wound. He nodded with satisfaction to see that apart from normal inflammation about the suture line, there was no indication of suppuration.

"I didn't tell you, Frank, but you are the first patient that I have used carbolic acid to clean the area and stop any putrefaction. It looks like it has worked."

"Don't mention putrefaction to me!" Frank said with mock indignation. "I am butcher, and putrefied meat is an insult to me. But I am glad to know that you have stopped me from turning rancid."

"Don't thank me, thank Professor Joseph Lister of Glasgow. He has been God's gift to surgery."

Once he had redressed the wound and washed his hands again, Logan prepared to go.

"Would you be able to send that young man who rescued me in the snow, Doctor?"

"Ah yes, young Billy Tanner," Logan mused. "Yes, I need to talk to him myself. I'll send him over to see you just as soon as I see him."

"Perhaps I could give him some reward?"

"Leave it to me, Frank. I have something in mind for Billy Tanner."

"And I wish I could give you a reward, Doctor Munro, for all this visiting that you do around town."

Logan shook his head dismissively. "Just pay my bill, Frank, that's all I ask. And assure Anna that you'll never do anything like this again."

***

Logan was disappointed to find that Martha Pomeroy was not at home when he called at her house. Instead, a notice was tacked to the door, saying that she was attending a lady in labor and that she was unsure when she would be back.

"Who can that be?" he mused to himself, for he was pretty sure that he knew all the pregnant women in Wolf Creek and he was not anticipating any of them going into labor over the Christmas period. Except Deputy Campbell's daughter, of course, and that birth had already come and gone.

Lighting his pipe, he trudged through the snow on the rest of his round.

Richard Wilhite, the owner of The Imperial Hotel, was in a good mood, despite the fact that his chef, Andre Duquesne, was confined to bed.

"Fortunately Leroy, the assistant chef, has picked up a lot from Andre and we can cope until he is back on his feet. I think he even seems a bit better today."

He laughed. "Maybe we ought to let you have a special room of your own, here, Doctor Munro. You are here often enough visiting hotel patients."

And indeed, when Logan called in on the French chef and found him resting in bed he was pleased to see that his swollen ankles had gone down and his heart rate had already slowed down.

"I can't say that I am overwhelmed by the taste of the medicine that you have prescribed for me, *docteur*," Andre said as Logan coiled his stethoscope into a bundle and replaced it in his black bag. "*Peut-être* you would like me to advise on some flavors you could add to them. A little aniseed, perhaps, or vanilla?"

Logan laughed. "I may just take you up on that, Andre."

"And have you been to see my friend Linus Zubriggin about your watch?"

"That's my last task before I head back for a late lunch"

"Well, speaking of food, perhaps I can cook you a special meal as a thank you for all that you are doing for me. You and a guest of your choice."

Logan smiled and left. A meal for two?

And he again started wondering where Martha Pomeroy could be.

***

Linus Zubriggin's shop had a fancy clock hanging outside it, out of reach of prying hands, although not out of reach of a gunshot, as witnessed by the two bullet holes through it from some over-imbibed reveler from Dogleg City one Saturday night. Remarkably, or perhaps a testimony to the watchmaker's skill, the bullets had not damaged the mechanism and it was reckoned to be the most accurate timepiece in Wolf Creek.

A bell tinkled as he opened the door and went in.

Logan had never actually been inside the shop before, or met Linus Zubriggin, and he was delightfully surprised to find himself in such an emporium that immediately stimulated several of his senses. There were clocks of all shapes and sizes on counters, on walls and in cabinets. There were also watches galore, and everywhere there was the ticking of time. There were also glorious smells of resins, woods and oils. And curiously, there was also a pleasant malty smell.

Yet, coming from the brightness of the snow into the dim interior, it took a few seconds to fully accustom himself to the different light. For some reason the shutters were down further than he would expect in December, and yet at a work table there was a bright oil lamp with a couple of mirrors set up to reflect light down onto a work surface. On the table, there was a clock, which was in the process of being dismantled, and above it a contraption with a levered large lens.

But there was no-one sitting at the desk.

Despite himself, Logan took a sharp intake of breath when his eye fell upon an empty glass on the desk, just outside the beamed light from the oil-lamp. Beside it, half empty ,was a bottle of *The Glenlivet* single malt whisky!

He found it hard to believe that anyone else in Wolf Creek had ever heard of the Scottish malt whisky, far less actually managed to get hold of a bottle.

And there were two bottles missing from his supply!

A bead curtain was swept aside and a small man of around the middle-sixties entered. He was wearing thick spectacles and a green eyeshade. He was wearing a starched collar and a necktie with a heavy green work apron on top, which had numerous streaks of oil upon it. He raised his hand to his eyeshade as if to further shield his eyes from the light outside.

Logan saw that he was screwing his eyes up to see him, despite the pebble glass spectacles. He was clean-shaven, albeit he had a fringe of hair low down on his neck, seemingly where his razor had missed sprouting stubble.

"Good afternoon. You are the town doctor, I think," he said, coming forward and offering his hand.

Logan noticed the slight tremor and smelled the whisky on his breath.

"Doctor Logan Munro," he said, shaking Linus's hand. "I see that you have kept out of my professional care, just as I have kept out of yours – until now."

"What do you mean!" Linus snapped.

Logan could see that he had touched a raw nerve and that the little Swiss was of an irritable nature. "Just that I need to see you to have my watch repaired."

He drew out his gold Hunter watch and detached the chain from his vest. "I need it to take pulses," he went on.

"But more importantly, it is of immense sentimental value. My wife gave it to me in India, when we were married." He could not keep the quaver from his voice whenever he mentioned Helen. "She passed away and I like to have it near me. And working."

The watchmaker took it from him and held it up close to his spectacles. Then he clicked his tongue, took off the spectacles, and screwed a watchmaker's loupe into his eye socket. He opened the watch, brought it up close to the loupe and peered at the dial.

"British made, by the look of it, so it probably has a lever escapement." He held it to his ear and wound it up, then shook his head. "I'd say that either the balance wheel or the lever escapement havegotten stuck. It should be fixable, but I'm afraid that I can't do it right now."

Logan felt a tinge of disappointment. "I can leave it."

Linus sensed Logan's disappointment. "I only mean that I can't get it done right away. My sight isn't too good right now, and my hands are a bit shaky. But when my grandson comes back I can get him to fix it."

The door opened behind Logan and the bell tinkled.

"Why, Doctor Munro, good to see you here, sir," came a young voice.

Logan turned to see Billy Tanner standing at the door with his hat in his hands. He saw the boy's nervous glance in the direction of the work table and the bottle of whisky.

"You are in luck, Doctor Logan," said Linus Zubriggin. "Speak of the devil. Here's my grandson right now."

Logan raised an eyebrow at Billy, but said nothing, for he had no desire to cause the boy embarrassment. "Your grandfather was telling me that you could fix my watch, Billy."

Billy swallowed hard and held his hand out to take the watch from his grandfather.

"I'll leave you to it for a while," Linus said. "Billy will take a look and tell you if he can fix it straight away, or if you will need to leave it."

When the watchmaker left, Billy slid onto the seat by the work bench and placed the watch on the table under the magnifying glass.

Logan watched him open it up and reach for a small rack containing an array of delicate tools.

He watched Billy fiddle with it, as if he was performing a delicate operation.

"Thank you for not saying anything in front of my grandfather, Doctor Munro,'" he said. He withdrew the tools, snapped the lid shut and then wound the watch. Immediately the second hand started to move. "The balance wheel had just slipped. It is as good as new."

"I am grateful," Logan said, taking it back and attaching the chain to his vest button before depositing the watch in his pocket. "Now tell me, why did you steal the whisky? Was it a Christmas present for your grandfather?"

"That's what I told him, sir," Billy replied. "But it wasn't that. That's why I took two bottles instead of one."

"I don't understand, Billy."

"I wanted you to find out and I wanted you to come here to complain to my grandfather."

"Actually, it was Frank Kloepfer the butcher, whom you found in the snow, who suggested that I come and see your grandfather, because my watch had stopped working. Me coming had nothing to do with the whisky."

"It d...didn't?"

"It doesn't really matter, since I am here now. The question is, why are you so keen to get me here? Is it because your grandfather drinks too much and is melancholic? Or is it because he's going blind?"

Billy looked up at him incredulously. "How did you know?"

"It is no great diagnostic challenge, Billy. He's a watchmaker and yet he has the shop almost in darkness. He has the thickest spectacle lenses, yet he can still barely see. And he's taught you to do all the fine, delicate work."

Billy nodded. "But he is stubborn and won't see you about it. I...I thought that if I could get you to come to him..."

The bead curtain was swept back and Linus came in. He looked cross. "I may be going blind, Billy, but there's nothing wrong with my hearing. I heard everything and..."

"And you are mad with me, Grandpa?" Billy said dejectedly.

"Of course not. I am proud of you, Billy. Proud that you have seen me sinking further and further into a whisky bottle and you did that for me. Even though there is nothing any doctor can do. I'm just old and have spent too many years fixing watches. I strained my eyes, Billy. I'm just going to go blind."

Then the old watchmaker sighed. "But I am sorry that you stole the whisky, Billy. I will pay you for the bottles, Doctor."

Logan put a hand on Linus's arm "Don't worry about that. Why don't you sit down and take that eyeshade and those spectacles off and let me be the judge of whether I can help or not? Let's not let Billy's wily plan go to waste."

It took a matter of a minute or two for Logan to diagnose the problem.

"You have cataracts in both eyes, Linus," he told the watchmaker. "That means that the lenses in your eyes have started to crystallize and have stopped the light getting in. Look Billy, you can see that the pupils of his eyes, which should be nice and black are almost white."

Billy took the magnifying glass that Logan handed him and looked closely at his grandfather's eyes. He gasped. "I see what you mean. I remember the lens of the bull's eye that you let me dissect at school. Is…is there anything that can be done?"

Linus shook his head. "There is nothing that can be done, Billy. I surely can't afford to go to any of those fancy hospitals back east."

Logan put a hand on his shoulder. "There is no need for that. The cataracts are both ripe, which means that they could be extracted. I could do one of them right here in Wolf Creek. And if that gives you back decent sight, then in a month or so I can do the other."

Linus's lower jaw dropped. "You could do that, Doctor Munro? When?"

"The sooner the better. This afternoon, if I can get hold of Martha Pomeroy."

***

Much to Logan's chagrin, and Linus's disappointment, Logan could not locate Martha.

"Why do you need Mrs. Pomeroy, Doctor Munro?" Billy asked when Logan returned to tell them the news.

"I have total faith in her," Logan replied. "She isn't squeamish and she does exactly what I tell her when I operate."

"I could do what you tell me, sir. I'm not squeamish and…and…"

"And I would like him to be there, Doctor," Linus said. "I won't be scared if Billy is there."

Logan smiled. "I have to admit that there is merit in that. Come on, we'll go over to my surgery right now."

***

After giving Linus an eighth of an ounce of chloroform through the perforated disc on top of the Chisolm inhaler that he used to administer the anesthetic, Logan checked Linus's pulse against his Hunter watch.

"It works just fine now," he said with satisfaction. "And your grandfather's pulse is good and strong. Now we have to move quickly, Billy. First, I am going to clean his eye with a boric acid eyewash. You just hold his eyelids open with this little eyelid retractor."

He inserted the instrument. "That's it. Now he won't be able to blink in his sleep. I'll just steady his eyeball, then I can make my incision."

Logan picked up a fine myrtiform, triangular shaped knife and made a small opening at the extreme lower margin of the cornea. Then, as he removed the blade, he used an even finer blunt-pointed, double-edged scalpel to widen the incision, before picking up a pair of fine, curved scissors to complete it in a half arc around the bottom of the cornea.

"In ancient days, back in India in the fifth century before our Lord was born, surgeons used to do this," he explained to the awestruck Billy. "But then they used to just shove a needle in and displace the lens into the vitreous cavity."

"The vitreous is the jelly at the back of the eye," Billy said with a grin. "I remember from the bull's eye."

Logan nodded approval. While he was impressed that the lad showed no signs of feeling squeamish, yet he was even more impressed that he had retained all that he had told him from the biology lesson. "Exactly so. But leaving it there could cause problems, so we are using the technique that a French surgeon called Jacques Daviel first did in Paris in 1748.

"Now we pick up this flap," he explained as he elevated the cornea with a small flat spatula. "And I open the front of the capsule of the lens."

Billy watched in amazement as over the next ten minutes Logan skillfully and patiently loosened the cataract and eased it out with a pair of fine forceps.

"And now we just replace the corneal flap, clean the eye again and then we'll put a dressing on it. Nature will heal it."

By the time Linus came round from the operation Logan had applied a compress and wound a bandage round his head to keep it secure.

"You are going to have to stay right here for twenty-four hours, Linus," Logan said. "I'll be taking the dressing off then, and we'll see if the operation has been a success."

149

The Swiss watchmaker nodded his head. "I can't believe how little it hurts. Now I'm just going to pray that it gives me some sight back."

"I'll pray with you, grandfather," Billy said.

Logan washed his hands and tidied his instruments away and then left them to it.

***

Billy stayed with his grandfather all of the next twenty-four hours and attended to all of his needs. They were both apprehensive when Logan came to remove the dressings.

"Heavens above!" Linus gasped as the eye compress was removed and he was able to blink his eye open. "I see light and colors that I haven't seen for years. Thank you, Doctor Munro. Thank you from the bottom of my heart."

Logan inspected the eye and nodded with satisfaction. "You're going to have to stay here another day, then we'll get you back home. But it will be resting in a chair for a week and I'll want you to wear smoked glass spectacles for a week. Your eye has to be allowed to heal up properly."

"Is it all right if I stay here again, Doctor Munro?" Billy asked.

"Of course, it is, Billy," Logan replied. Then to Linus:

"You have no lens in the eye anymore, but with magnifying glasses and decent spectacles, you'll find a huge difference. Then we can look at doing the other eye."

"It is a good thing that I have Billy to help me, then," Linus said, beaming at his grandson. "He has a good pair of hands and will make an excellent watchmaker."

Logan noticed the look of disappointment on Billy's face.

150

"Actually, Linus, I agree about his hands. And the way he just helped me I would say that in a few years, as long as he completes his education, he could become a surgeon if he wanted."

Billy's eyes went wide with amazement. "Do you really think so, Doctor Munro?"

"I think you are capable of it, Billy."

Linus stared at Logan. "My grandson? A surgeon? You...you think?"

"I do, and maybe all that has happened lately has been a sign that's what he's meant to do in life."

"But what about money?" Billy asked. "Doesn't it cost a fortune to become a surgeon?"

"You can start saving, Billy. Working at jobs where folk will give them." He grinned. "And if I were you, I'd start by asking Frank Kloepfer the butcher f he needs any help. He's already kind of anxious to thank you for saving his life."

Linus's jaw dropped in amazement. "Billy saved the butcher's life?"

Logan laid a hand on Billy's shoulder. "There seems to be a lot about this remarkable young man that you don't yet know about, Linus."

Linus nodded. "I think I am beginning to learn, Doctor Munro."

***

Logan finally managed to find Martha Pomeroy two days later. He asked her to have dinner with him at the Imperial Hotel on New Year's Eve. Richard Wilhite had arranged for them to be served in a private room off the main restaurant.

151

"You look tired, Logan," she said as they sat opposite each other enjoying the meal especially cooked for them by Andre Duquesne, who felt better than he had for months, and which showed in the fulsomeness and flavor of his food.

"Yes, it has been a hard Christmas season for me professionally," he replied. "I have had a number of difficult and challenging cases."

He held her gaze. "And I couldn't find you. I had to operate on Linus Zubriggin'scataract, and I had hoped that you would assist me."

Matha bent her head. "I…I'm sorry, Logan. I had a difficult….a difficult…"

"You are not going to say you had a difficult confinement are you, Martha? I read the note you left on your door, but as far as I am aware no-one in Wolf Creek is due imminently, nor have I heard that there has been a birth."

She looked up at him. "I am sorry, I made that up. I was…frightened."

"Frightened, Martha? Of me?"

"I was scared of what you wanted to ask me. You know that I lost Thomas in the war. Well, it is just that I can't…I couldn't…I am not ready for anything."

Logan reached across and laid a hand on hers. "Nor am I, Martha. I think we both have feelings for each other, but I, too, am wounded. I haven't gotten over Helen. I'm not ready either – yet."

Martha did not remove her hand, but she sighed with relief. "Then what did you want to ask me?"

"As I just said, I have had a difficult few days and I have been visiting folks all over town. I sincerely believe that what this town needs now is a hospital. I plan to have a word with Mayor Dab Henry and some of the other most influential folk and see if we can't get things started. I could do with a proper operating theater, a ward for patients and some help."

He smiled. "That is where you come in, Martha. I wondered if you would be interested in being my nurse?"

She slid her hand from under his and sipped some water. "I think that is a splendid idea, and if it comes to fruition, I would be delighted. It would give me real purpose. It is just a pity that you cannot get anyone to help you. You seem to always be delivering babies, patching up gunshot wounds or operating on folk. Lord knows when you get time to sleep."

They laughed, then over the dessert Logan told her about Billy Tanner.

"I think that young man needs to be encouraged," he said as he finished eating and dabbed the corners of his mouth with his napkin. "He could make an excellent watchmaker, but I think he could be an even better surgeon. For a fifteen-year-old he showed great promise. He wasn't flustered or upset when I operated on his grandfather's eye."

Andre Duquesne entered, bearing a tray upon which were two glasses and a bottle of *The Glenlivet.*

"Your whisky, as arranged, Doctor Munro. It is my hope that you have both enjoyed your dinner?"

Logan effusively complemented him on the meal, as did Martha, and Andre poured them each a glass of the amber malt whisky.

"It may be a couple of hours early," Logan said when the delighted Andre had left them alone again. "In my country Hogmanay is an important night. We see out the old year and usher in the next. And a fine malt whisky like *The Glenlivet* is used to toast it in. I had this specially sent over from Scotland. So let us raise a glass together in the hope that one day soon Wolf Creek will have a hospital."

"And that we work together," she added.

"Good friends, Martha."

They clinked glasses.

"Always, Logan.Always."

THE END

O DEADLY NIGHT

Troy D. Smith

The lawmen of Wolf Creek had their Christmas dinner at the county jail. Extra chairs had been brought in, and the city and county peace officers gathered around G.W. Satterlee's desk. Food was piled high on it, prepared by Stephanie "Ma" Adams, and tin plates and utensils clattered as the men dug in. Mayor Dab Henry had supplied several tankards of beer, though not without a public shaming from Sam Gardner—Dab didn't like to spend money if he could help it.

Several of the men had already had hearty holiday meals earlier in the day, but did their level best to share in the Christmas spirit by consuming just a little more. Sheriff Satterlee himself had enjoyed a fine repast at the Norwood Dairy, invited to stay for the meal after he came to arrest several of Andrew Rogers' troublemaking cowhands. Sheriff's deputy Laban Campbell had eaten with his own family, but came to the jail dinner out of a sense of camaraderie—for one thing, he was too much the New England Calvinist to go in for extended revelry. For another, he was distracted by thoughts of his daughter Emmy, who had given birth the day before, and whose condition had been an embarrassment for the Campbell family.

Deputy Sheriff Bill "Zack" Zacherly and Deputy Marshal Quint Croy sat together in a corner. They were both young men with no families and no ties, and had become close friends since taking on their respective

155

badges. Laban Campbell, in fact, was the only Wolf Creek lawman who had a family. Deputy Marshal Seamus O'Connor had still enjoyed a convivial holiday, having attended the first midnight Mass performed by the town's new Catholic priest Father Sean Flannery, then celebrating with a light meal earlier that day with the *padre* and Ben Tolliver (and son.)

Town marshal Samuel Horace Gardner, like Zack and Quint, had no celebration other than this one. Much as he liked to keep up a cynical, crusty shell –which was almost completely sincere –Christmas made him a little wistful. He sure as hell didn't miss Illinois –but he did find himself thinking about his ma, wondering how she was getting on, and about a young woman with billowing red hair he had promised once to marry. He pushed those thoughts down, but they had kept trying to bob their heads back above the surface over the course of the day, like kittens that refused to be drowned. He had tried to distract himself that afternoon by a trip to Abby Potter's whorehouse, but neither Abby nor any of his favorites were there, so he didn't stay.

This, then, was his family. The picture was completed by the grizzly-like snores of town drunk Rupe Tingley emanating from his cell. Rupe had drunk himself into his usual stupor after a hearty Christmas meal with the farmer Hutch Higgins and his family.

Satterlee stood and lifted his beer. "If we could stop shoveling food into our faces for a minute," he said, "I have a toast. Here's to two good men, Spence Pennycuff and Fred Garvey, who were in our company here this time last year... both shot down in their prime by the Danby Gang."

"May their souls rot in hell," Campbell said. "The Danby Gang, that is,"

"Amen," Sam said.

"They were good men," Satterlee repeated. "Laban, Seamus, I wish you could have known 'em. Anyways—here's to *auld lang syne.*"

"Hear, hear," Seamus said.

Satterlee sighed. "All right, then," he said after taking a deep gulp of suds. "Let's go back to shovelin' it in."

"Hear, *hear*," Zack said with a grin.

They had not been returned to their eating long when the front door flew open and Rob Parker, the bartender at the Lucky Break, rushed in.

"Somebody better come quick," he said, "there's trouble."

"It's Christmas," Sam said. "Let the drunks at the Lucky Break, and every other saloon, carve each other up, it would bring me yuletide cheer."

"There's drunks and carvin', all right," Parker said, "but it ain't at the saloon. We're shut down, and I went on home. No, this is out by my place. It's that damn troublemaker Elijah Lusk. He's beatin' the hell out of his wife and kids, right out in the street, and wavin' a butcher knife around sayin' he's gonna kill 'em."

Sam stood with a sigh. "I was finished up anyways," he said. "You boys continue on your culinary course. I'll go whack this miscreant and be back before you can say Bob's-your-uncle. And believe me, I aim to crack his skull good. It'll be my Christmas present to the world."

157

Sam grabbed his wolf-headed walking stick and headed for the door. "You go on home to the bosom of your family, Rob. Don't entertain any notions about stabbin' 'em, neither, my charity only goes so far."

"Give 'em hell, Sam," Satterlee said, then returned his attention to his ham.

"Damn straight I will," Sam muttered as he stepped out into the cold night.

The cold cut through him as he trudged down the street. He wished he'd had the good sense to wrap up in the buffalo robe the sheriff kept by his door, and that the snow would quit piling up so damn high. He was definitely going to make this quick.

A small crowd had gathered around the Lusk family, although at a safe distance. Leave it to the sterling citizens of Wolf Creek to come out in the snow on Christmas night if it meant getting to see a drunk carve on his children.

"Please, Lige," Ruthie Lusk begged from her prone position in the snow. Her mouth was bleeding, and her face was already bruised and swelling. Lusk stood over her, brandishing the knife; their two young sons, Caleb and Joe, huddled together a few feet away. "Please, Lige, stop it!"

"Shut up!" Lige said in a thickly slurred voice. "I told you, by God, you better not burn my taters one more time, not on Christmas! You done it on purpose, to spite me!"

"Quit it, Pa," one of the boys said. Sam could never tell them apart.

"Shut up, runt," the boy's father answered, "you'll get yours next."

158

Suddenly the boy flew from the ground like a bird, launching himself at Lusk. The drunk backhanded him practically in mid-air, and he tumbled into a snowbank.

"Here now," Sam called out. "That's enough."

Lusk stared at the marshal. "Mind your own business, Gardner."

"Afraid this is my business, hoss."

One of the bystanders laughed. "Aw, Elijah is just still sore over how that tiny schoolmarm buffaloed him a couple weeks back, shootin' the hat right off his head. I reckon he's too yellow to go lookin' for her!"

A great howl erupted from Lusk's throat, and came tearing out into the night air. He threw his head back and continued the cry, his face to the moon; the timbre of his roar changed subtly from rage to despair.

Sam stared at the bystander who had taunted the drunk. "Carl Avery," Sam said. "Keep your mouth shut, or *you're* next on *my* list."

While the marshal was distracted, Elijah Lusk burst into action every bit as swiftly as his son had. He grabbed his wife by the hair and jerked her to him, jabbing the knife at her throat. Its tip drew blood from her flesh. His hand shook, and his wife whimpered like an animal in a trap.

The Lusk children begged their father for mercy on their mother, but he gave no sign of hearing them.

"I won't take no more sass from this witch," Lusk said, "cuttin' me down with her eyes ever' day, like I was no more'n a dog. Like I'm no good and won't never be no good."

"You just ease off, Lige," Sam said. "A minute ago you were looking at a thrashing and a night in jail. Don't you make me shoot you dead, in front of your boys, on Christmas."

"I told her, don't burn them taters again," Lusk mumbled distantly. "Not on Christmas. Just this once, just this once I wanted things to all go right, to be good. I begged her, marshal, I begged her."

"I have some taters back at the office," Sam said, his voice as soothing as he could make it.

But then he saw the shadow on Elijah Lusk's face. The cold shadow, spread up from his soul, darkening his eyes and indicating –with a quick intake of breath –that he was about to plunge the blade deep into his wife's throat.

And Sam Gardner released the death that was always held in check, awaiting his split-second command. The revolver blazed in the night, its bullet catching Lusk right between the eyes and exiting the back of his skull, taking brain and bone with it, spreading the bloody gore across the snow. Lusk's body, already dead, flew backward and he released the grip on his wife; the butcher knife furrowed her flesh but did not sink into her windpipe, and she fell immediately to the side, screaming.

Smoke curled from Sam's weapon. Lusk's body twitched. Ruthie Lusk's scream turned into a sob. Everyone else was still as death.

Sam dimly realized that Rob Parker was standing beside him.

"Damn," the bartender said. "Shit like this'll sap the joy right outta Christmas."

The Lusk boys arose and stumbled through the snow, tumbling onto their father's body. Ruthie climbed onto the pile as well. They were all sobbing piteously, calling out to the dead man.

One of the boys raised his tear-stained face to the marshal. "You killed him! You killed my pa!"

"I'm sorry, son," Gardner said. "I saved your ma, though."

Ruthie's face was twisted now with rage, as her sons' were. Both boys looked like miniature versions of their hateful father.

"You didn't have to kill him!" the mother said. "Oh, my poor, poor Lige! He was drunk, he didn't know what he was doing!"

"He never liked my pa!" the other boy said, choking on the words. "He coulda just wounded him, but he *wanted* to kill him!"

"I didn't…"

The second boy launched himself at the marshal, just as his brother had done earlier at their father.

"I hate you! I hate you!" Sam held the boy away, but his small fists pummeled the marshal's arms. "I'll grow up and I'll kill you, just like you killed my pa, see if I don't!"

Rob Parker pulled the boy away, which was not an easy task, and held him.

"You best go on back to your Christmas dinner, Marshal," Rob said. "I'll go by Gravely's and tell him he has a fresh body to bury. He'll treat me like I was Santy Claus."

Sam walked back down the street, much more slowly than he had come. He bypassed the jail, and his friends, and went to his own office instead. He pulled a half-empty bottle of bourbon out of his desk and drank it all without his mind forming a coherent thought. He thought he could still hear the wails of the mourning family, but it might have been the wind.

***

Six days passed. No pint-sized assassins tried to bushwhack him, and the town got back to normal –if such a word could ever be applied to Wolf Creek. At least no one else was shot dead in the intervening time, making Elijah Lusk the last person to die in the town in 1871.

Sam Gardner sat alone on one of the stone benches on Boot Hill, looking over the graves. He puffed languidly on a long cigar. It was still snowing, hard as ever, and felt even colder than it had on Christmas. This time Sam had brought a buffalo robe, and was wrapped tightly in it. He watched the snowflakes swirl through the air, chasing each other. It was too dark, and too snowy, to read the names on the tombstones –but Sam knew who they were. Every one.

Someone approached him from the darkness.

"I hope I am not disturbing you, Marshal," Doc Munro said. The bowl of his Meerschaum pipe glowed cherry red.

Sam looked up at him. "If I'm disturbed, Doc, it's none of your doing."

"I did not expect to find anyone up here this time of night. If you seek solitude, I quite understand."

"I don't seek it, exactly, it just follows me around. Have a seat if you like."

Logan Munro sat beside the marshal. The doctor chuckled softly.

"Certainly a morbid place to ring in the new year," Munro said. "I suppose that speaks volumes about our respective characters."

"I did the same thing last year," Sam said. "But the place is a lot bigger now."

Sam waved with his cigar. "Yonder lies that poor young school teacher and the little Chinese boy, both killed by the Danby Gang. And my deputy Fred, a damn good man. Then that other kid, the one that got shot in the crossfire from Andrew Rogers' thugs."

He pointed in the other direction. "And good old Edith Pettigrew.Annoying even in death. She stood near this very spot and told me and G.W. we were letting this town go to hell, and everybody in it was liable to wind up dead because of us. And lo and behold, there she is."

"I owe you an apology, Marshal."

"For what?"

"I assumed you were here because you were haunted by the lives you've been forced to take this year, and that perhaps you were here to bid their ghosts fly away with the old calendar. But you're here for the same reason I am; to say goodbye to the souls of those you could not save."

Sam grunted. "I have done my part in moving the real estate, that's true enough. But I don't have any regrets on that mark. Except, in some cases, I regret I didn't shoot 'em sooner, or shoot more of their friends. Except maybe Elijah Lusk –I regret that the damned fool made me shoot him in front of his kids on Christmas. But I attribute that to a character flaw on his part, not mine."

Sam took a deep breath. "But that pretty little schoolmarm. I see her in my dreams. I kind of wish we'd had Cora Sloane as schoolteacher then; she'd've whipped out that horse-pistol of hers and picked off half the gang. She's more man than just about anybody in this town. I'm tempted to deputize her, except we need her to control those damned kids."

Munro chuckled. "She is quite capable."

Sam puffed on his cigar. "So you're here to feel sorry for yourself about your failures, too, then."

The doctor nodded. "Yes. I've helped move this real estate, as you put it, quite a bit as well."

"Yeah, but there's a big difference," Sam said. "For every patient up here you lost, there's ten or twenty that you saved. That's good arithmetic, and you should be proud of it, not ashamed of the few that slipped through the cracks."

"Do you really believe that?" Munro asked.

"Yes, I really do."

"Then you should realize, Marshal, that the same holds true for you. For every person in here you couldn't save, there are several more who *would* be here if not for you."

Sam blew a smoke ring. "So be it, Doc, you have me convinced. We're a couple of goddamned saints. Only reason we ain't been canonized is we're still breathing."

"I'm glad you've agreed to see reason," Munro said cheerfully. He produced a bottle from beneath his own thick robe. "I have just a touch of the old *Glenlivit* here," he said. "Finest Scotch in the world. I had planned to have one final toast to the good people who have left us –but there is enough left for us both to send them off appropriately."

"Then by all means, let's have at it."

Munro lifted the bottle. "May God's peace and mercy go with you all, dear souls. We've wander'd mony a weary fit sin' auld lang syne."

"Damn straight," Sam said.

Munro took a deep draught, then handed it to the marshal, who drank the rest and passed the bottle back to the doctor. They sat awhile in silence.

"And here's to 1872," Sam said at length. "It has got to be a more peaceful year in Wolf Creek than the last one has been."

"Amen to that," Doctor Munro said.

They both knew it was not very likely.

THE END

About the Authors:

JAMES J. GRIFFIN I've had a great interest in the West and particularly Texas Rangers from when I was a kid, so it was natural when I started writing the Rangers would be the subject of my novels. Over the years I've accumulated enough knowledge about the Rangers to be considered an amateur historian of the organization. I also amassed a large collection of Texas Ranger artifacts, which are now in the permanent collections of the Texas Ranger Hall of Fame and Museum in Waco. I recently wrote a ten issue series of short stories for High Noon Press. These are ebooks, titled A Ranger Named Rowdy, A Texas Ranger Tim Bannon Story. All are currently available, and a Christmas "A Ranger Named Rowdy" novella will be released in both electronic and print versions in early December. My short story "The Toys" was a finalist for the 2012 Peacemaker Award for best short story.

My other great passion in life is horses, especially Paints. I've owned horses most of my life, and currently own an American Paint Horse named Yankee. He is a Pet Partners certified therapy animal, and we make visits to local hospitals and nursing homes. In addition, Yank and I are members of the Connecticut Horse Council Volunteer Horse Patrol. We act as auxiliary park rangers, patrolling state parks and forests.

I'm a native New Englander, and as much as I love the West I love New England, particularly my adopted home state of New Hampshire, even more. Currently, I divide

166

my time between Branford, Connecticut and Keene, New Hampshire.

To learn more about my books, and see some of Yankee's tricks, check out my website at www.jamesjgriffin.net .

JERRY GUIN aka J L Guin Wolf Creek book 9, *A Wolf Creek Christmas* is keeping the series alive and fresh. I am proud to have my story included. Other publications this year include "Asa Pepper's Place" in Wolf Creek 6, The eBook "Justified" and the novella "Charlie's Money" by High Noon Press. I also have a story in the La Frontera anthology *Dead or Alive. Drover's Bounty*, my Black Horse Western, was released by Robert Hale on August 30. On the horizon is *The Bandit*, my entry into the West of The Big River series by Western Fictioneers, Also coming up is another novella, "Crossroads Fast Gun" by High Noon Press. I live in Northern California in the mountains with my editor wife Ginny. I would like to wish everyone a Merry Christmas.

MEG MIMS Award-winning author Meg Mims lives in Michigan with her husband and two dogs (one of them the 'hero' of her novella, *Santa Paws*). *Double Crossing*, a western historical mystery, won the WWA 2012 Spur Award for Best First Novel. Meg published the sequel, *Double or Nothing*, in 2013. She is also one-half of the writing team of D.E. Ireland for St. Martin's Press with a cozy mystery series coming out in 2014. Meg enjoys gardening, crafts, watercolor painting - anything but housework.

CLAY MORE I was born in St Andrews, Scotland, and Clay More is actually my western pen name. My real name is Keith Souter and I live in England within arrow-shot of the ruins of a medieval castle, the scene of two of my historical novels. I am a part time doctor, medical journalist and novelist, writing in four different genres - crime, historical, YA and westerns. I also enjoy the challenge of short fiction for which I have won a couple of prizes, including a 2006 Fish Award for my story *The Villain's Tale*.

My medical background finds its way into a lot of my writing, as can be seen in most of my western novels and short stories. My character in Wolf Creek is Doctor Logan Munro, the town doctor, who is gradually revealing more about himself with each book he appears in. Another of my characters is Doctor Marcus Quigley, dentist, gambler and bounty hunter who is appearing as a monthly eBook short story, published by High Noon Press. I am a member of various writers' organisations, including Western Fictioneers and Western Writers of America. If you care to find out more about me, visit my website: http://www.keithsouter.co.uk

Or my blog http://moreontherange.blogspot.co.uk

CHERYL PIERSON

A native Oklahoman, I live in Oklahoma City and write historical westerns and western romance. My Wolf Creek character, Derrick McCain, who is featured in "It Takes a Man," is also included in *WC Book 1: Bloody Trail,* and *WC Book 5: Showdown at Demon's Drop.* Look for more about Derrick and his half-brother, Carson Ridge, in the exciting WC Christmas anthology coming this fall, and thanks for dropping in on the citizens of Wolf Creek! My short story, "The Keepers of Camelot," included in the Western Fictioneers' Christmas anthology *Six Guns and Slay Bells: A Creepy Cowboy Christmas*, was nominated for the 2013 Western Fictioneers Peacemaker Award in the short story category. I also have a new release, *Kane's Chance*, that will appeal to all ages. It's a coming-of-age story of a young boy in the old west, a novel you won't want to miss.

JACQUIE ROGERS I'm a country girl at heart, raised on a dairy farm in Idaho — a great place to grow up. My friend and I rode our horses all over the Owyhee Mountains and managed to get ourselves in just about every sort of pickle. Now I live in the suburbs of Seattle with my husband who is also my cheerleader (sans pompoms) and proofreader. I write in several genres including fantasy romance, and YA fantasy, but mostly western historical romance. My latest release is **Sleight of Heart**. The fourth book in my award-winning *Hearts of Owyhee* series, **Much Ado About Miners**, will be released later this month.

I love to hear from readers! Please visit my website, http://www.JacquieRogers.com, sign up for my newsletter at http://eepurl.com/qhA_1, or join the fun at the Pickle Barrel Bar & Books at Facebook, https://www.facebook.com/groups/JacquieRogers/. I also wrangle the popular western blog, Romancing The West, http://romancingthewest.blogspot.com.

JORY SHERMAN began his literary career as a poet in San Francisco's famed North Beach in the late 1950s, during the heyday of the Beat Generation. His poetry and short stories were widely published in literary journals when he began writing commercial fiction. He has won numerous awards for his poetry and prose and was nominated for a Pulitzer Prize in Letters for his novel, Grass Kingdom. He won a Spur Award from Western Writers of America for The Medicine Horn. He has also won a number of awards from the Missouri Writers Guild, and other organizations. Sherman was a book producer, packaging books for many major publishers, including Avon, Bantam, Berkley, Paperjacks, Pinnacle, Harlequin Gold Eagle, Zebra, and others. His CHILL series of mysteries, published by Pinnacle, appeared in 14 countries. He has published more than 400 books since 1965, more than 1000 articles and 500 short stories. In 1995, Sherman was inducted into the National Writer's Hall of Fame. He lived in the Ozarks for over 20 years, last making his home in Branson. His writing regularly appears in The Ozarks Mountaineer and Ozarks Monthly his latest collection of Ozarks pieces are in The Hills of Home, published by Hardshell Word Factory. He now lives on a lake in northeast Texas. His latest novels, The Dark Land, Sunset Rider and Texas Dust were published by Berkley. The first novel in his new series, THE

OWLHOOT TRAIL, <u>Abilene Gun Down</u> was published by Pocket Books on June 1^{wt,} 2004. He recently completed writing 2 new series for Berkley, THE VIGILANTE, and THE SAVAGE GUN. He also just completed writing a series for Harper Collins, THE SHADOW RIDER. He wrote 2 novels under the name of his deceased friend, Ralph Compton: <u>The Palo Duro Trail</u> and <u>The Ellsworth Trail</u> for Signet. His latest novel in The Baron series, THE BARON HONOR, , was published by Forge Books in January, 2005. His collection of Ozarks short stories, published by AWOC in trade paperback, THE SADNESS OF AUTUMN. Recently AWOC published two new short story collections, LITTLE JOURNEYS, with an introduction by Richard S. Wheeler, and SHADOWS OF YESTERYEAR, a collection of western stories with an introduction by Loren D. Estleman. Jory painted the cover of The Alamo for this one. Sherman recently completed THE ABILENE TRAIL for Signet, a Ralph Compton Trail Drive book, SAVAGE VENGEANCE for Berkley, in his Savage Gun series, and DEATH RATTLE, also for Berkley, in his Sidewinder series. Literary critics consider Sherman to be among the top 5 of western writers, according to Dale Walker, historian. Warren French, former professor of literature at the University of Florida, wrote that: "Jory Sherman has a strange and powerful knowledge of language and an almost perfect ear." Sherman continues to write novels and short stories as well as conduct writing workshops. He lives in Pittsburg, Texas with his wife, Charlotte. www.jorysherman.com

TROY D. SMITH hails from Sparta, Tennessee. His first Western story appeared in *Louis L'Amour Western Magazine* in 1995; in 2001 his novel *Bound for the Promise-Land* won the Spur Award. He earned his Ph.D. at the University of Illinois and teaches at Tennessee Tech. As a professional historian his primary fields are American Indians, slavery, and the South; as a historical novelist, his interests lie in the human beings at the heart of his stories. "I don't write about things that happen to people, I write about people that things happen to." www.troyduanesmith.com

CHARLIE STEEL, Tale-Weaver Extraordinaire, is a novelist and internationally published author of short stories. Steel credits the catalyst for his numerous books and hundreds of short stories to be the result of being a voracious reader, along with having worked at many varied and assorted occupations. Some of his experiences include service in the Army, labor in the oil fields, in construction, in a foundry, and as a salvage diver. Early in his life he was recruited by the US Government and spent five years behind the Iron Curtain. Steel's work has been recognized and reviewed by various publications and organizations including Publisher's Weekly, Western Fictioneers, and Western Writers of America. Steel holds five degrees including a PhD. He continues to read, research, and collect western literature. He is the author of Desert Heat, Desert Cold, and Other Tales of the West. Charlie Steel lives on an isolated ranch at the base of Greenhorn Mountain, in Southern Colorado.

www.charliesteel.net

CHUCK TYRELL I've read westerns all my life. The first one I remember was Smokey, by Will James. I read everything I could find, living far away from the west in Japan. In 1979, I wrote a western novel for a Louis L'Amour write-alike contest. Didn't win. Decided I could not write fiction. The typewritten manuscript occupied a bottom desk drawer until 2000. I dusted it off and edited it as I input it into a computer file. Sent it off to a publisher, Robert Hale Ltd., in London. They bought it providing I'd cut it down to 40,000 words. The novel is now known as *Vulture Gold*, the first of the Havelock novels.
Besides awards in advertising and article writing, a short story won the 2010 Oaxaca International Literature Competition and my novel *The Snake Den* won the 2011 Global eBook Award for western fiction. Other than that, I just write westerns and fantasy. My home is in Japan, where I live with one wife and one dog and one father-in-law, visited quite often by daughters and grandkids. I write most of my fiction by longhand, usually at Starbucks. Other writing I do on the laptop. My website is www.chucktyrell.com and my blog is www.chucktyrell-outlawjournal.blogspot.com I have a number of short stories lying around in various anthologies.

BIG JIM WILLIAMS "I love the Old West's history and stories," says Big Jim Williams, who sold his first western story, "Buckshot's Thanksgiving," to Western

Horseman Magazine in 1998. His The Old West audio
book was included in The Best of Westerns (year 2000)
package with Jack London, Louie L'Amour, Owen Wister
and Bill Brooks. He narrated his second book, Tall Tales
of The Old West (2001). He's written westerns for
Frontier Tales, Rope And Wire, Cardroom Poker News,
Shoot!, Livestock Weekly, American West, SNIPLITS,
and for the 2013 anthology, Dead or Alive (La Frontera
Publishing). He's loved westerns since attending
Depression-era 12 cent Saturday matinees and watching
Hopalong Cassidy destroy evildoers and help the good
guys. After a lifelong radio career, Big Jim became a
professional publicist writing hundreds of press releases
that "often bordered on fiction." He's also been published
in OverMyDeadBody, Orchard Press Mysteries, Suspense,
Writers' Journal, Radio World, Writers Weekly, and the
anthologies, At Home and Abroad: Prize-Winning Stories;
Murder to Mil-Spec, and The Last Man, with Ray
Bradbury, London, and Poe. He and his writing wife, Joan,
have two sons, and four grandchildren. Big Jim loves
writing, watching western movies, drinking beer, and
napping in California.

Find them all here!:http://amzn.to/15ez8f6

NEW! Featuring three years' worth of Peacemaker Award winners and finalists!

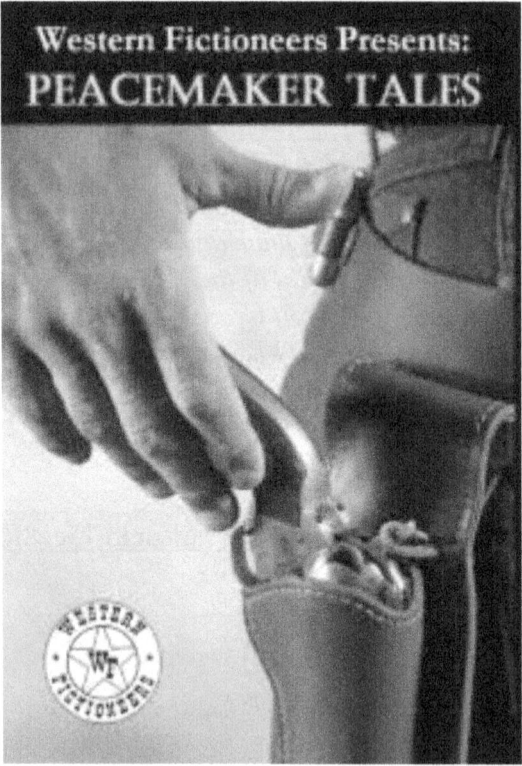

Also from Western Fictioneers:

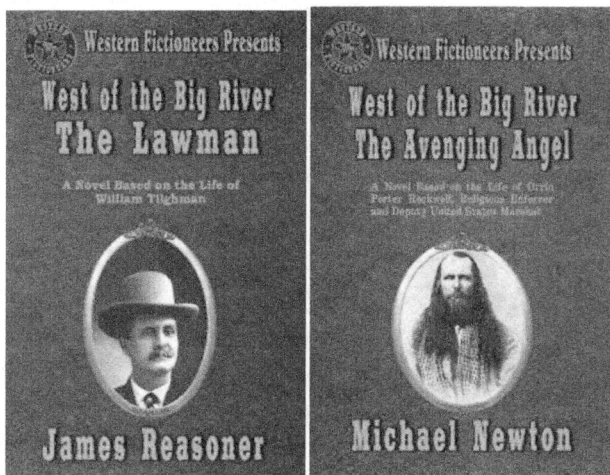

www.westernfictioneers.com

Western Fictioneers

Made in the USA
Monee, IL
30 August 2025